Fawcett Gold Medal Books
in the Travis McGee Series
by John D. MacDonald

THE DEEP BLUE GOOD-BY
NIGHTMARE IN PINK
A PURPLE PLACE FOR DYING
THE QUICK RED FOX
A DEADLY SHADE OF GOLD
BRIGHT ORANGE FOR THE SHROUD
DARKER THAN AMBER
ONE FEARFUL YELLOW EYE
PALE GRAY FOR GUILT
THE GIRL IN THE PLAIN BROWN WRAPPER
DRESS HER IN INDIGO
THE LONG LAVENDER LOOK
A TAN AND SANDY SILENCE
THE SCARLET RUSE
THE TURQUOISE LAMENT
THE DREADFUL LEMON SKY
THE EMPTY COPPER SEA
THE GREEN RIPPER
FREE FALL IN CRIMSON

the
deep
blue
good-by

john d. mac donald

fawcett gold medal • new york

A Fawcett Gold Medal Book
Published by Ballantine Books
Copyright © 1964 by John D. MacDonald Publishing, Inc.

ISBN 0-449-12673-0

Manufactured in the United States of America

First Fawcett Gold Medal Edition: May 1964
First Ballantine Books Edition: December 1983

uno

IT was to have been a quiet evening at home.

Home is the *Busted Flush*, 52-foot barge-type houseboat, Slip F-18, Bahia Mar, Lauderdale.

Home is where the privacy is. Draw all the opaque curtains, button the hatches, and with the whispering drone of the air conditioning masking all the sounds of the outside world, you are no longer cheek to jowl with the random activities aboard the neighbor craft. You could be in a rocket beyond Venus, or under the icecap.

Because it is a room aboard, I call it the lounge, and because that is one of the primary activities.

I was sprawled on a deep curve of the corner couch, studying charts of the keys, trying to work up enough enthusiasm and energy to plan moving the *Busted Flush* to a new mooring for a while. She has a pair of Hercules diesels, 58 HP each, that will chug her along at a stately six knots. I didn't want to move her. I like Lauderdale. But it had been so long I was wondering if I should.

Chookie McCall was choreographing some fool thing. She had come over because I had the privacy and enough room. She had shoved the furniture out of the way, set up a couple of mirrors from the master stateroom, and set up her rackety little metronome. She wore a faded old rust-red leotard, mended with black thread in a couple of places. She had her black hair tied into a scarf.

She was working hard. She would go over a sequence time and time again, changing it a little each time, and when she was satisfied, she would hurry over to the table and make the proper notations on her clip board.

Dancers work as hard as coal miners used to work. She stomped and huffed and contorted her splendid and perfectly proportioned body. In spite of the air conditioning, she had filled the lounge with a faint sharp-sweet odor of large overheated girl. She was a pleasant distraction. In the lounge lights there was a highlighted gleam of perspiration on the long round legs and arms.

"Damn!" she said, scowling at her notations.

"What's wrong?"

"Nothing I can't fix. I have to figure exactly where everybody is going to be, or I'll have them kicking each other in the face. I get mixed up sometimes."

She scratched out some notes. I went back to checking the low tide depths on the flats northeast of the Content Keys. She worked hard for another ten minutes, made her notes, then leaned against the edge of the table, breathing hard.

"Trav, honey?"

"Mmm?"

"Were you kidding me that time we talked about . . . about what you do for a living?"

"What did I say?"

"It sounded sort of strange, but I guess I believed you. You said if X has something valuable and Y comes along and takes it away from him, and there is absolutely no way in the world X can ever get it back, then you come along and make a deal with X to get it back, and keep half. Then you just . . . live on that until it starts to run out. Is that the way it is, really?"

"It's a simplification, Chook, but reasonably accurate."

"Don't you get into a lot of trouble?"

"Sometimes yes, sometimes no. Y is usually in no position to make much of a fuss. Because I am sort of a last resort, the fee is fifty per cent. For X, half is a lot better than nothing at all."

"And you keep it all sort of quiet."

"Chook, I don't exactly have business cards printed. What would I say on them? Travis McGee, Retriever?"

"But for goodness' sake, Trav, how much work like that can you find laying around when you start to get so broke you need it?"

"So much that I can pick and choose. This is a complex culture, dear. The more intricate our society gets, the more semi-legal ways to steal. I get leads from old clients sometimes. And if you take a batch of newspapers and read with great care, and read between the lines, you can come up with a fat happy Y and a poor X wringing his hands. I like to work on pretty good-sized ones. Expenses are heavy. And then I can take another piece of my retirement. Instead of retiring at sixty, I'm taking it in chunks as I go along."

"What if something came along right now?"

"Let's change the subject, Miss McCall. Why don't you take some time off, and make Frank highly nervous, and we'll assemble a little group and cruise a little houseboat party on down to Marathon. Let's say, four gentlemen and six ladies. No drunks, no whiners, nobody paired off, no dubious gender, no camera addicts, nobody who sunburns, nobody who can't swim, nobody who . . ."

"Please, McGee. I'm really serious."

"So am I."

"There's a girl I want you to talk to. I hired her for the group a couple of months ago. She's a little older than the rest of us. She used to dance, and she's working back into it very nicely, really. But . . . I really think she needs help. And I don't think there's anyone else she can go to. Her name is Cathy Kerr."

"I'm sorry, Chook. I've got enough right now to last for months. I work best after I begin to get nervous."

"But she thinks there is really an awful lot involved."

I stared at her. "She thinks?"

"She never got to see it."

"I beg your pardon?"

"She got a little drunk the other night and very weepy, and I've been nice to her, so she blurted it all out to me. But she should tell you herself."

"How could she lose something she never saw?"

Chookie wore that little fisherman smile which means the hook has been set. "It's really too complicated for me to try to explain. I might mess it up. Would you just do this, Travis? Would you talk to her?"

I sighed. "Bring her around sometime."

She padded lithely over to me and took my wrist and looked at my watch. Her breathing had slowed. Her leotard was sweat-dark and fitted her almost as closely as her healthy hide.

She beamed down at me. "I knew you'd be nice about it, Trav. She'll be here in twenty minutes."

I stared up at her. "You are a con artist, McCall."

She patted my head. "Cathy is really nice. You'll like her." She went back to the middle of the lounge and started her metronome again, studied her notations, and went back to work, leaping, thumping, making small grunts of effort. Never sit in the first row at the ballet.

I tried to get back to channel markers and tide levels, but all concentration was gone. I had to talk to the woman. But I was certainly not going to be shilled into some nonsense project. I had the next one all lined up, waiting until I was ready. I had enough diversions. I didn't need more. I was sourly amused that Chook had wondered where the projects came from. She was living proof they popped up all the time.

Promptly at nine there was a bing-bong sound from the bell I have wired to a push button on the pier piling. If anybody should ignore the bell, step over my chain and come down my gangplank, the instant they step on the big rope mat on the transom deck there is an ominous and significant bong which starts many abrupt protective measures. I have no stomach for surprises. I have endured too many of them. They upset me. The elimination of all removable risk is the most plausible way of staying alive.

I flicked on my rear deck lights and went out the aft doorway of the lounge, Chookie McCall gasping behind me.

I went up and unsnapped the chain for her. She was a sandy blonde with one of those English schoolboy haircuts, where the big eyes look out at you from under a ragged thatch of bangs. She had overdressed for the occasion, the basic black and the pearl clip and the sparkly little envelope purse.

In explosive gasps Chook introduced us and we went inside. I could see that she was elderly by Chook's standards. Perhaps twenty-six or -seven. A brown-eyed blonde, with the helpless mournful eyes of a basset hound. She was a little weathered around the eyes. In the lounge lights I saw that the basic black had given her a lot of good use. Her hands looked a little rough. Under the slightly bouffant skirt of the black dress were those unmistakable dancer's legs, curved and trim and sinewy.

Chookie said, "Cathy, you can go ahead and tell Travis McGee the whole bit, like you told me. I've finished up, so I'll leave you alone and go back and take that bath, if it's okay, Trav."

"Please do take a bath."

She gave me a pretty good rap behind the ear and went off and closed the master stateroom door behind her.

I could see that Catherine Kerr was very tense. I offered her a drink. She gratefully accepted bourbon on ice.

"I don't know what you can do," she said. "Maybe this is silly. I don't know what anybody can do."

"Maybe there isn't a thing anybody can do, Cathy. Let's just start by assuming it's hopeless and go on from there."

"I drank too much one night after the last show and told her and I guess I shouldn't have been telling anybody."

In her light, nasal voice I could detect some of that conch accent, that slightly sing-song way the key people talk.

"I'm married, sort of," she said defiantly. "He took off three years ago and I haven't heard a thing from him. I've got a boy age of five, and my sister keeps him, down at the home place on Candle Key. That's why it's stinking, not so much for me as the boy Davie. You want a lot for a kid. Maybe I dreamed too much. I don't know, rightly."

You have to let them get to it their own way.

She sipped her drink and sighed and shrugged. "The way it happened, I was nine years old. That was in nineteen forty-five. That was when my daddy came home from the war. Sergeant David Berry. That's my maiden name, Catherine Berry. I named my boy after him, even though my daddy had been in prison a long long time when the boy was born. What I think happened, my daddy got onto some way of making money when he was overseas in World War Two. A lot of money, I think. And he found some way of bringing it back. I don't

know how. He was over there in India and
Burma. He was gone over two years. He was a
drinking man, Mr. McGee, and a strong man
and he had a temper. He came back on a ship
and got off it in San Francisco. They were going to send him to some place in Florida to get
discharged, and he was coming home. But in
San Francisco he got drunk and killed another
army man, and because he thought they would
keep him and he wouldn't see us at all, he cut
and ran. And he got all the way home. Running like that didn't do him any good at the
trial. It was a military trial, like they have. He
came home in the middle of the night, and
when we got up he was out there on the dock,
just looking at the water. It was a foggy day.
He told my mother what happened. He said
they were going to come and get him. I have
never seen a woman cry like that, before or
since. They came and got him like he said, and
they put him in prison for life in Leavenworth,
Kansas. It was an officer he killed. My mother
took a bus out there to see him that Christmas, and every Christmas from then on until
he died two years ago. When there was enough
money, she'd take along me or my sister. I got
to go twice. My sister went out there three
times."

She went off into dreaming and memories.
In a little while she gave a start and looked at
me and said, "I'm sorry. The way it was, he
thought he would get out sooner or later. I
guess they would have let him out, but there

was always some kind of trouble coming up. He wasn't a man to settle down to prison like some can. He was a very proud man, Mr. McGee. But here is the thing I have to tell you. Before they came and got him. I was nine. My sister was seven. He sat on the porch with his arms around us, and he told us all the wonderful things that would happen when they turned him loose. We'd have our own boats and our own horses. We would travel all over the world. We would have pretty dresses for every day in the year. I always remembered that. When I was older, I remembered it to my mother. I thought she might make fun. But she was serious enough. She told me I was never to talk about it to anybody. She said my father would work things out in his own way, and some day everything would be fine for all of us. But of course it never was. Last year a man came to us, name of Junior Allen. A smiling man. He said he had spent five long years in that place and knew my daddy well. And he knew things about us he could only know if my daddy told him. So we were glad to see him. He said he had no family of his own. A freckledy smiling man, quick to talk and good with his hands at fixing things. He came in with us, and he got work over at the Esso station, and the money helped. My mother was started sick then, but not so sick she couldn't care for the kids by day, when Christine—that's my sister—and I were working. Her two, and my boy Davie, three little kids. It would have neatened out better if Junior Allen had took up with Christine, her husband being killed by the hurricane of sixty-one, when the cinderblock wall of the Candle Key Suprex blew over onto him. Jaimie Hasson his name was. We've had all this bad luck with our men." She tried to smile.

"Sometimes it comes in bunches."

"Lord knows we've had a bunch. It was me Junior Allen liked best. By the time we took up together, my mother was too sick to care too much. As she got sicker she seemed to turn inward like some people do, not noticing much. Christine knew what was going on between us, and she told me it was wrong. But Junior said the way Wally Kerr took off and left me, I was as good as divorced. He said I couldn't even ask for a divorce until seven years went by without hearing from Wally. I since found out he lied.

"I lived like man and wife with Junior Allen, Mr. McGee, and I loved that man. When Mother died, it was good to have him close. It was near Christmas. She was washing greens, and she just bent over the sink and made a little kitten sound and slid down dying and she was gone. Christine stopped her job because somebody had to be with the kids, but with me and Junior Allen working, there was just enough to get by. There was one thing strange in all that time he was with us. I thought it was because he had gotten so close to my

daddy in prison. He liked to talk—about
Daddy. He never stopped asking questions
about him—about what things he liked to do
and what places he liked to go, almost as if he
was trying to live the same life my daddy had
lived 'way before the war, when I was as little
as Davie is now. Now I remember other things
that didn't seem as strange then as they do
now. I remembered about the fish shack my
daddy built on a little no-name island, and I
told Junior Allen, and the next day he was off
he was gone all day in the skiff, and he came
back bone tired and grouchy. Little things like
that. I know now that he was hunting, Mr.
McGee. He was hunting whatever my daddy
hid, whatever it was he brought back that was
going to give us those dresses and horses and
around the world. Using one excuse and
another, he managed to dig up just about
every part of the yard. One day we awoke and
Junior Allen was gone. That was near the end
of this last February, and both the markers by
our old driveway were tumbled down. My
daddy built them long ago of coquina rock too
big and grand for such a little driveway, but
built rough. Junior Allen tumbled them down
and away he went, and in the ruin of the one
on the left was something I don't know what it
was to start. Scabs of rust and some rotten
cloth that was maybe once army color, and
some wire like a big clip, and some rust still in
the length of a little chain, and something that

could have once been some kind of a top to something.

"He took along his personal things, so I knew it was just like Wally Kerr all over again. No good looking for him. But he showed up again three weeks later, on Candle Key. Not to see me. He came back to see Mrs. Atkinson. She's a beautiful woman. She has one of the big new houses there, and I guess he met her when he was working at the Esso and putting gas in her Thunderbird car. People told me he was staying in her house, and that he'd come down in expensive clothes and a big boat of his own and moved right in with her. They would tell me and then look at me to see what I'd say or do. The fourth day he was there I came upon him in the town. I tried to speak and he turned around and hurried the other way, and I shamed myself, running after him. He got into her car and she wasn't there and he was pawing his pockets and cursing because he couldn'tfind the key, his face ugly. I was crying and trying to ask him what he was doing to me. He called me a busted-down little slut and told me to go back and hide in the swamp where I came from, and he roared away. Enough people saw it and enough heard it, so it gave them a lot to talk about. His boat was right there, a big cruiser, registered to him and owned by him, right at Mrs. Atkinson's dock, and she closed the house and they went off in it. Now I know she lived careful, and couldn't buy him a boat like that. And I know that living with us, Junior Allen didn't have one dollar extra. But he looked and looked and looked and found something and went away and came back with money. But I can't see there's a thing in the world anybody can do about it. Chookie said tell you, so I've told you. I don't know where he is now. I don't know if Mrs. Atkinson knows, if she isn't still with him someplace. And if anybody could find him, what could they do?"

"Was there a name and port of registry on the boat?"

"Called it the *Play Pen*, out of Miami. Not a new boat, but the name new. He showed a couple of people the papers to prove it his. I'd say it was a custom boat, maybe thirty-eight foot, white topsides, gray hull and a blue stripe."

"Then you left Candle Key."

"Not long after. There just wasn't enough money with just one of us working. When I was little a tourist lady saw me dancing alone and gave me free dancing lessons every winter she came down. Before I was married I danced two years for pay up in Miami. So I came back into it and it's enough money so I can send Christine enough and she can get along. I didn't want to be in Candle Key any more anyway."

She looked at me with soft apologetic brown eyes, all dressed in her best to come talk to me. The world had done its best to subdue and humble her, but the edge of her good tough spirit showed through. I found I had taken an irrational dislike to Junior Allen, that smiling man. And I do not function too well on emotional motivations. I am wary of them. And I am wary of a lot of other things, such as plastic credit cards, payroll deductions, insurance programs, retirement benefits, savings accounts, Green Stamps, time clocks, newspapers, mortgages, sermons, miracle fabrics, deodorants, check lists, time payments, political parties, lending libraries, television, actresses, junior chambers of commerce, pageants, progress, and manifest destiny.

I am wary of the whole dreary deadening structured mess we have built into such a glittering top-heavy structure that there is nothing left to see but the glitter, and the brute routines of maintaining it.

Reality is in the enduring eyes, the unspoken dreadful accusation in the enduring eyes of a worn young woman who looks at you, and hopes for nothing.

But these things can never form lecture materials for blithe Travis McGee. I am also wary of all earnestness.

"Let me do some thinking about all this, Cathy."

"Sure," she said, and put her empty glass aside.

"Another drink."

"I'll be getting along, thank you kindly."

"I can get in touch through Chook."

"Sure."

I let her out. I noticed a small and touching thing. Despite all wounds and dejections, her dancer's step was so firm and light and quick as to give a curious imitation of joy.

dos

I wandered through the lounge and tapped at the door and went into the master stateroom. Chook's fresh clothing was laid out on my bed, and her sodden stomp-suit was in a heap on the floor. I heard her in the tub, wallowing and sloshing and humming.

"Yo," I said toward the half-open door.

"Come in, darling. I'm indecent."

The bathroom was humid with steam and soap. The elderly Palm Beach sybarite who had ordered the pleasure barge for his declining years had added many nice touches. One was the tub, a semi-sunken, pale blue creation a full seven feet long and four feet wide. Chook was stretched out full length in it, her black

21

hair afloat, bobbing around in there, creamy with suds, utterly luxuriant. She beckoned me over and I sat on the wide rim near the foot of the tub.

I guess Chook is about twenty-three or -four. Her face is a little older than that. It has that stern look you see in old pictures of the plains Indians. At her best, it is a forceful and striking face, redolent of strength and dignity. At worst it sometimes would seem to be the face of a Dartmouth boy dressed for the farcical chorus line. But that body, seen more intimately than ever before, was incomparably, mercilessly female, deep and glossy, rounded—under the tidy little fatty layer of girl pneumatics—with useful muscle.

This was a special challenge, and I didn't know the terms, knew only that most of the time they are terms one cannot ultimately afford, not with the ones who, like Chook, have their own special force and substance and requirements. She had created the challenge, and was less bold with it than she wanted me to believe.

"How about that Cathy?" she said, her voice elaborately casual.

"A little worn around the edges."

"How not? But how about helping her?"

"There's a lot to find out first. Maybe too much. Maybe it would be too long and too expensive finding out what I'd have to find out."

"But you couldn't tell about that until you looked into it."

"I could just make à guess."

"And not do anything."

"What's it to you, Chook?"

"I like her. And it's been rough."

"The wide world is full of likable people who get kicked in the stomach regularly. They're disaster-prone. Something goes wrong. The sky starts falling on their head. And you can't reverse the process."

She sloshed a little and scowled. My left hand was braced on the edge of the tub. Suddenly she lifted a long steaming gleaming leg and put the soaking sole of her bare foot firmly on the back of my hand. She curled her toes around the edge of my wrist in a strange little clasp and said, her voice husky and her eyes a little alarmed at her own daring, "The water's fine."

It was just a little too contrived. "Who are you trying to be?"

She was startled. "That's a funny thing to say."

"You are Chookie McCall, very resolute and ambitious and not exactly subject to fits of abandon. And we have been friends for a couple of months. I made my pass, 'way back when, and you straightened me out very pleasantly and firmly. So who are you trying to be? Fair question?"

She took her foot away. "Do you have to be such a bastard, Trav? Maybe I was having a fit of abandon. Why do you have to question things?"

"Because I know you, and maybe there are enough people getting hurt."

"What is that supposed to mean?"

"Chook, dear girl, you are just not trivial enough for purely recreational sex. You are more complex than that. So this very pleasant and unexpected invitation has to be part of some kind of a program or plan of action or design for the future."

Her eyes shifted just enough to let me know I had struck home. "Whatever it was, darling, you've bitched it good."

I smiled at her. "If it's pure recreation, dear, without claims or agreements or deathless vows, I'm at your service. I like you. I like you enough to keep from trying to fake you into anything, even though, at the moment, it's one hell of a temptation. But I think you would have to get too deeply involved in your own justifications because, as I said, you are a complex woman. And a strong woman. And I am no part of your future, not in any emotional way." I stood up and looked down at her. "Now you know the rules, it's still your decision. Just holler."

I went back to the lounge. I examined my sterling character and wondered if it would be functional and entertaining to thud my head against the wall. My fingernails made interesting little grooves in the palms of my hands. My ears grew, extending to tall hairy points, and as I did a little pacing, they kept turning in her direction, listening for a shy summons.

When at last she came out, she wore white slacks and a black blouse, with her dark damp hair bound in a red scarf. She carried her dancing gear in a little canvas case. She looked tired and shy and rueful, and came slowly to me, meeting my glance with a multitude of little quick glances of her own. Clothing leans her, disguising ripeness.

I cupped my hand on her chin and kissed a soft, warm and humble Indian mouth. "What was it all about?" I asked her.

"A fight with Frank. Kind of a nasty one. So I guess I was trying to prove something. Now I feel like a fool."

"Don't."

She sighed. "But I would have felt worse the other way. I guess. Eventually. So thanks for being smarter about me than I am."

"My friend, it wasn't easy."

She scowled at me. "What's the matter with me? Why can't I be in love with you instead of him? He's really a terrible man. He makes me feel degraded, Trav. But when he walks into the room, sometimes I feel as if I'll faint with love. I think that's why ... I feel so sympathetic toward Cathy. Frank is my Junior Allen. Please help her."

I told her I would think about it. I walked her to her little car, out in the sweet hot night, and watched her go sputtering off, carrying

the ripeness, unimpaired, back to surly Frank.
I listened for the roar of applause, fanfare of
trumpets, for the speech and the medal. I
heard the lisping flap of water against the hull,
the soft mutter of the traffic on the smooth
asphalt that divides the big marina from the
public beach, bits of music blending into nonsense, boat laughter, the slurred harmony of
alcohol, and a mosquito song vectoring in on
my neck.

I kicked a concrete pier and hurt my toes.
These are the playmate years, and they are
demonstrably fraudulent. The scene is reputed
to be acrawl with adorably amoral bunnies to
whom sex is a pleasant social favor. The new
culture. And they are indeed present and
available, in exhausting quantity, but there is
a curious tastelessness about them. A woman
who does not guard and treasure herself cannot be of very much value to anyone else. They
become a pretty little convenience, like a guest
towel. And the cute little things they say, and
their dainty little squeals of pleasure and
release are as contrived as the embroidered in-
itials on the guest towels. Only a woman of
pride, complexity and emotional tension is
genuinely worth the act of love, and there are
only two ways to get yourself one of them.
Either you lie, and stain the relationship with
your own sense of guile, or you accept the in-
volvement, the emotional responsibility, the

permanence she must by nature crave. I love you can be said only two ways.

But tension is also a fact of life, and I found myself strolling toward the big rich Wheeler where the Alabama Tiger maintains his permanent floating house party. I was welcomed with vague cheers. I nursed a drink, made myself excruciatingly amiable, suitably mysterious and witty in the proper key, and carefully observed the group relationships until I was able to identify two possibles. I settled for a blooming redhead from Waco, Takes-us, name of Molly Bea Archer, carefully cut her out of the pack and trundled her, tipsy and willing, back to the *Busted Flush*. She thought it an adorable little old boat, and scampered about, ooing and cooing at the fixtures and appointments, kittenish as all get out until faced with the implacable reality of bedtime, then settled into her little social chore with acquired skill and natural diligence. We rested and exchanged the necessary compliments, and she told me of her terrible problem—whether to go back to Baylor for her senior year, or marry some adorable little old boy who was terribly in love with her, or take a wonderful job in Houston working for some adorable little old insurance company. She sighed and gave me a sisterly little kiss and a friendly little pat, and got up and went and fixed her face and crammed herself back into her

shorts and halter, and after I had built two fresh
drinks into the glasses we had brought from the
other craft, I walked her back to the Tiger's
party and stayed fifteen more minutes as a small
courtesy.

When I was alone in darkness in my bed, I
felt sad, ancient, listless and cheated. Molly
Bea had been as personally involved as one of
those rubber dollies sailors buy in Japanese
ports.

And in the darkness I began to remember
the brown and humbled eyes of Cathy Kerr,
under that guileless sandy thatch of hair.
Molly Bea, she of the hard white breasts
lightly dusted with golden freckles, would
never be so humiliated by life because she
could never become as deeply involved in the
meaty toughness of life. She would never be
victimized by her own illusions because they
were not essential to her. She could always
find new ones when the old ones wore out. But
Cathy was stuck with hers. The illusion of
love, magically changed to a memory of
shame.

Maybe I was despising that part of myself
that was labeled Junior Allen. What an
astonishment these night thoughts would
induce in the carefree companions of blithe
Travis McGee, that big brown loose-jointed
boat bum, that pale-eyed, wire-haired
girl-seeker, that slayer of small savage fish,
that beach-walker, gin-drinker, quip-maker,
peace-seeker, iconoclast, disbeliever, argufier,

that knuckly, scar-tissued reject from a structured society.

But pity, indignation and guilt are the things best left hidden from all the gay companions.

Take them out at night.

McGee, you really know how to live, old buddy.

Adorable little old buddy.

It was to have been a quiet evening at home. Until Cathy Kerr came into it, bringing unrest. At last I could admit to myself that the rubbery little adventure with the Takes-us redhead was not because I had denied myself a sudsy romp with Chook, but because I was trying to ignore the challenge Cathy had dropped in my lap. I could afford to drift along for many months. But now Cathy had created the restlessness, the indignation, the beginnings of that shameful need to clamber aboard my spavined white steed, knock the rust off the armor, tilt the crooked old lance and shout huzzah.

Sleep immediately followed decision.

tres

THE next morning, after making laundry arrangements, I untethered my bike and pedaled to the garage where I keep Miss Agnes sheltered from brine and sun. She needs tender loving care in her declining years. I believe she is the only Rolls Royce in America which has been converted into a pickup truck. She is vintage 1936, and apparently some previous owner had some unlikely disaster happen to the upper half of her rear end and solved the problem in an implausible way. She is one of the big ones, and in spite of her brutal surgery retains the family knack of going eighty miles an hour all day long in a kind of ghastly silence. Some other idiot had her repainted a horrid electric blue. When I found her squatting, shame-faced, in the back row of a gigantic car lot, I bought her at once and named her after a teacher I had in the fourth grade whose hair was that same shade of blue.

Miss Agnes took me down the pike to Miami, and I began making the rounds of the yacht brokers, asking my devious questions.

After a sandwich lunch, I finally found the outfit that had sold it. Kimby-Meyer. An Ambrose A. Allen, according to their record sheet, had bought a forty-foot Stadel custom back in March. They had his address as the Bayway Hotel. The salesman was out. A man named Joe True. While I waited for him to come back, I phoned the Bayway. They had no A. A. Allen registered. Joe True got back at two-thirty, scented with good bourbon. He was a jouncy, leathery little man who punctuated each comment with a wink and a snicker, as if he had just told a joke. It saddened him somewhat to learn I was not a potential customer, but he brightened up when I offered to buy him a drink. We went to a nearby place where he was extremely well known by all, and they had his drink in front of him before we were properly settled on the bar stools.

"Frankly, I didn't know he was a live one," Joe True said. "You get to know the look of people buy boats like that one. That Mr. Allen, he looked and acted more like hired crew, like he was lining something up for his boss. Grease under his fingernails. A tattoo on his wrist. A very hard-looking character, very brown and wide and powerful-looking. And smiling all the time. I showed him a lot of listings, and he was so quick to talk price I began to take him serious. He settled on that *Jessica III*, that was the name the original owner registered her at."

"A good boat?"

"A fine boat, Mr. McGee. She's had a lot of use but she was maintained well. Twin 155's, and they'd been overhauled. A nice compromise between range and speed. Nicely appointed. Built in fifty-six if I remember right. Good hull performance in a rough sea. We took it out. He handled it and liked it. When we came back in, he scared hell out of me. I thought we were going to peel away about fifty feet of dock. But he hit the reverse just right, and I was up in the bow, and he put me right beside a piling as gentle as a little girl's kiss. And when he checked the boat over, he knew just what to look for. He didn't need any survey made. And he bought it right. Twenty-four thousand even."

"Cash?"

Joe True shoved his glass toward the bartender and looked at me and said, "You better tell me again what it is you're after."

"I'm just trying to locate him, Joe. As a favor for a mutual friend."

"I got a little nervous about that deal, and I told Mr. Kimby about being nervous and he checked it out with his lawyer. No matter where Allen got the money, nobody can come back on us."

"Why did the money make you nervous?"

"He didn't look or act like the kind of a man to have that kind of money. That's all. But how can you tell? I didn't ask him where he got it. Maybe he's some kind of eccentric captain of finance. Maybe he's thrifty. What he had was five cashier's checks. They were all from different banks, all from New York banks. Four of them were five thousand each, and one was twenty-five hundred. He made up the difference in hundred dollar bills. The agreement was we'd change the name the way he wanted and handle the paper work for him and do some other little things for him, nothing major, get the dinghy painted, replace an anchor line, that sort of thing. While that was being done our bank said the checks were fine, so I met him at the dock and gave him the papers and he took delivery. That man never stopped smiling. Real pale curly hair burned white by the sun and little bright blue eyes, and smiling every minute. The way he handled the boat, I finally figured he was actually buying it for somebody else, even though it was registered to him. Maybe some kind of a tax deal or something like that. I mean it looked that way because of the way those cashier's checks were spread around. He was dressed in the best, but the clothes didn't look just right on him."

"And you haven't seen him since?"

"Haven't seen him or heard from him. I guess he was a satisfied customer."

"How old would you say he is?"

Joe True frowned. "It's hard to say. If I had to guess, I'd say about thirty-eight. And in great shape. Very tough and quick. He jumped off that thing like a cat and he had the stern line and the spring line all rigged while I was making the bow line fast."

I bought Joe his third drink and left him there with his dear friends. Junior Allen was beginning to take shape. And he was beginning to look a little more formidable. He had left Candle Key in late February with something of value, and had gone to New York and managed to convert it into cash, all of it or some of it, whatever it was. Weeks later he had returned to Miami, bought himself a good hunk of marine hardware and gone back to Candle Key to visit the Atkinson woman. It had required considerable confidence to go back. Or recklessness. A man with a criminal record shouldn't flaunt money, particularly in an area where an angry woman might be likely to turn him in.

Yet, actually, the boat procedure was pretty good. It gave him a place to live. With papers in order and a craft capable of passing Coast Guard inspection, he wasn't likely to be asked too many embarrassing questions. People who build a transient life around a forty-foot cruiser are presumed innocent. I'd found the *Busted Flush* to be a most agreeable headquarters for the basically rebellious. You escape most of the crud, answer fewer questions, and you can leave on the next tide.

But there was one hitch, and perhaps Junior Allen wouldn't be aware of it. The tax people take a hearty interest in all registered craft over twenty feet. They like to make sure they weren't purchased with their money. A cash transaction like that one might intrigue some persistent little man up there in Jacksonville, and give him a heady desire to have a chat with Ambrose A. Allen, transient.

But first he would have to find him.

I wondered if I would find him first.

I visited the Bayway Hotel. It was a mainland hotel, small, quiet and luxurious in an understated way. The little lobby was like the living room in a private home. A pale clerk listened to my question and drifted off into the shadows and was gone a long time. He came back and said that A. A. Allen had stayed with them for five days last March and had left no forwarding address. He had given his address when registering as General Delivery, Candle Key. He had been in 301, one of their smallest suites. We smiled at each other. He smothered a yawn with a dainty fist and I walked out of his shadowy coolness into the damp noisy heat of the Miami afternoon.

The next question was multiple choice. I did not want to get too close to Junior Allen too soon. When you stalk game it is nice to know what it eats and where it drinks and where it beds down, and if it has any particularly nasty habits, like circling back and pursuing the pursuer. I did not know all the questions I wanted to ask, but I knew where to look for answers. Cathy, her sister, Mrs. Atkinson, and perhaps some people out in Kansas. And it might be interesting to locate somebody who had served with Sergeant David Berry in that long ago war. Apparently the Sergeant had found himself a profitable war. It was past four o'clock, and I kept thinking of questions I wanted to ask Cathy, so I headed on back toward my barge. I parked Miss Agnes handy to home, because I would need her that evening to go see Cathy Kerr.

I stripped to swim trunks and did a full hour of topsides work on the *Busted Flush,* taking out a rotted section of canvas on the port side of the sun deck, replacing it with the nylon I'd had made to order, lacing the brass grommets to the railing and to the little deck cleats, while the sun blasted me and the sweat rolled off. One more section to go and I will have worked my way all around the damned thing, and then I am going to cover the whole sun deck area with that vinyl which is a clever imitation of teak decking. Maybe, after years of effort I will get it to the point where a mere forty hours a week will keep it in trim.

I acquired it in a private poker session in Palm Beach, a continuous thirty hours of intensive effort. At the end of ten hours I had been down to just what I had on the table, about twelve hundred. In a stud hand I stayed with deuces backed, deuce of clubs down, deuce of hearts up. My next three cards were the three, seven and ten of hearts. There were three of us left in the pot. By then they knew how I played, knew I had to be paired, or have an ace or king in the hole. I was looking at a pair of eights, and the other player had paired on the last card. Fours. Fours checked to the eights and I was in the middle, and bet the pot limit, six hundred. Pair of eights sat there and thought too long. He decided I wasn't trying to buy one, because it would have been too clumsy and risky in view of my financial status. He decided I was trying to look as if I was buying one, to get the big play against a flush, anchored by either the ace or king of hearts in the hole. Fortunately neither of those cards had showed up in that hand.

He folded. Pair of fours was actually two pair. He came to the same reluctant conclusion. I pulled the pot in, collapsed my winning hand and tossed it to the dealer, but that hole card somehow caught against my finger and flipped over. The black deuce. And I knew that from then on they would remember that busted flush and they would pay my price for my good hands. And they did, for twenty more hours, and there were many many good hands, and there was a great weight of old-time money in that little group. In the last few hours I loaned the big loser ten thousand against that houseboat, and when it was gone I loaned him ten more, and when that was gone I loaned him the final ten and the craft was mine. When he wanted another ten, with his little Brazilian mistress as security, his friends took him away and quieted him down and the game ended. And I named the houseboat in honor of the hand which had started my streak, and sold the old *Prowler* on which I had been living in cramped circumstances.

After the manual labor, I treated myself to a tepid tub and a chilly bottle of Dos Equis, that black Mexican beer beyond compare, and dressed for summer night life. Just at dusk Molly Bea came a-calling, tall glass in hand, tiddly-sweet, pinked with sunburn, bringing along a dark lustrous giggler to show her my adorable little old boat. The giggler was named Conny, and she was from Gnaw-luns rather than Takes-us, but she was a similar piece, styled for romps and games, all a girlish prancing, giving me to believe—with glance and innuendo—that she had checked me out with Molly Bea, given her total approval, then matched for me and won. She was prepared to move in with me and send Molly Bea back to the Tiger. After the inspection tour, I got rid of both of them, locked up and went off to a downtown place which sells tourist steaks at native prices, and then went on out to the Mile O'Beach, to the Bahama Room, your host Joey Mirris, featuring for Our Big Summer Season, the haunting ballads of Sheilagh Morraine, and Chookie McCall and her Island Dancers. Closed Mondays.

Joey Mirris was a tasteless brassy purveyor of blue material and smutty sight gags. It was a pickup band, very loud and very bored. Shelagh Morraine had a sweet, true, ordinary little voice, wooden gestures and expressions, and an astounding 42-25-38 figure she garbed in show gowns that seemed knitted of wet cobwebs. But Chook and her six-pack were good. She planned the costumes, lighting, arrangements, routines, picked the girls carefully and trained them mercilessly. They were doing three a night, and the dancers were the ones bringing in the business, and Adam Teabolt, the owner-manager, knew it.

The room will take about two and a quarter, and they had about seventy for the eight o'clock show. I found a stool at the end of the raised bar, tried not to notice Mirris and Morraine, and then gave my full attention to the so-called Island Dancers. The wardrobe for the entire seven could have been assembled in one derby hat. Under the blue floods I saw Cathy Kerr working in perfect cadence with the group, wearing a rather glassy little smile, her body trim and nimble, light and muscular and quick. There is no flab on good dancers. There is no room for it, and no time to acquire it. Effort coats the trained golden flesh with little moist highlights. As always, the bored band did its best for the Chook-troop, and part of the routine was a clever satire on all sea-island routines.

After the eight o'clock show I sent a note back to Cathy and then went to the hotel coffee shop. She joined me five minutes later, wearing a dreary little blouse, a cheap skirt and her heavy stage make-up. We had a corner table. Through the glass wall I could see the lighted pool and the evening swimmers.

"I'm going to try to see if I can do anything, Cathy."

The brown eyes searched my face. "I surely appreciate it, Mr. McGee."

"Trav. Short for Travis."

"Thank you, Trav. Do you think you can do anything?"

"I don't know. But we have to make some kind of agreement."

"Like what?"

"Your father hid something and Junior Allen found it. If I find out what it is or was and where he got it, maybe there is somebody it should go back to."

"I wouldn't want anything that was stole."

"If I can make recovery of anything, Cathy, I'll take any expenses off the top and split what's left with you, fifty fifty."

She thought that over. "I guess that would be fair enough. This way, I've got nothing at all."

"But you can't tell anyone we have this arrangement. If anybody asks you anything about me, I'm just a friend."

"I think maybe you are. But what about those expenses if you don't get anything back?"

"That's my risk."

"So long as I don't end up owing. Lord God, I owe enough here and there. Even some to Chookie."

"I want to ask you a few questions."

"You go right ahead, Trav."

"Do you know of anybody who served with your father in the Army?"

"No. The thing is, he wanted to fly. He enlisted to try to get to fly. But he was too old or not enough schooling or something. He enlisted in nineteen forty-two. I was six years old when he went away. He trained in Texas someplace, and finally he got into the ... something about Air Transit or something."

"ATC? Air Transport Command?"

"That was it! Sure. And he got to fly that way, not flying the airplanes, but having a regular airplane to fly on. A crew chief he got to be. Over in that CBI place. And he did good because we got the allotment and after he was over there, those hundred dollar money orders would come once in a while. Once there were three of them all at once. Ma saved what she could for when he got back, and the way it turned out, it was a good thing she did."

"But you don't know anybody he served with?"

She frowned thoughtfully. "There were names in the letters sometimes. He didn't write much. My mother saved those letters. I don't know if Christy threw them out when she died. Maybe they're still down at the house. There were names in them sometimes."

"Could you ride down there with me tomorrow and find out?"

"I guess so."

"I want to meet your sister."

"Why?"

"I want to hear what she has to say about Junior Allen."

"She'll say she told me so. She didn't like him much. Can I tell my sister what you're trying to do for us?"

"No. I'd rather you wouldn't, Cathy. Tell her I'm just a friend. I'll find some way to get her to talk about Allen."

"What can she tell you?"

"Maybe nothing. Maybe some things you didn't notice."

"It'll be good to see my Davie."

"Why was Allen sent to prison?"

"He said it was a big misunderstanding. He went in the Army and he was making it his career. He was in the Quartermaster, in the part that they have boats, like the Navy. But little boats. Crash boats, they call the ones he was on. And then he got into the supply part of it, and in nineteen fifty-seven they got onto him for selling a lot of government stuff to some civilian company. He said he did a little of it, but not as much as they said. They blamed it all on him and gave him a dishonorable discharge and eight years at Leavenworth. But he got out in five. That's where he was a cellmate of my daddy, and said he came to help us because my daddy would have wanted him to. That's the lie he told us."

"Where did he come from originally?"

"Near Biloxi. He grew up on boats, that's how the Army put him into the boats. He said he had no folks left there."

"And you fell in love with him."

She gave me a strange and troubled look. "I don't know as it was love. I didn't want him to have me like that, right there at the home place with my mother still alive then, and Davie there, and Christine and her two. It was shameful, but I couldn't seem to help myself. Looking back I can't understand how it could be. Trav, I had a husband, and there was one other man beside my husband and Junior Allen, but my husband and the other man weren't like Junior Allen. I don't know how to say it to a stranger without shaming myself more. But maybe it could help somehow to know this about him. The first time or so, he forced me. He would be tender and loving, but afterward. Saying he was sorry. But he was at me like some kind of animal, and he was too rough and too often. He said it had always been like that with him, like he couldn't help himself. And after a while he changed me, so that it didn't seem too rough any more, and I didn't care how many times he came at me or when. It was all turned into a dream I couldn't

quite wake up from, and I went around feeling
all soft and dreamy and stupid, and not caring
a damn about what anybody thought, only caring that he wanted me and I wanted him. He's
a powerful man, and all the time we were
together he never did slack off. Do a woman
that way and I think she goes off into a kind of
a daze, because really it's too much, but there
was no way of stopping him, and finally I
didn't want to, because you get used to living
in that dazy way. Then when he come back
and moved in with that Mrs. Atkinson . . . I
couldn't stop thinking how . . ." She shook
herself like a wet puppy and gave me a shame-
faced smile and said, "How to get to be a damn
fool in one easy lesson. I was just something
real handy for him while he was looking for
what my daddy hid away. And all the time I
thought it was me pleasing him." She looked
at the coffee-shop clock. "I have to be going to
get ready for the next show. What time do you
want to go in the morning?"

"Suppose I pick you up about nine-thirty?"

"I'd rather I come to your boat about then, if
that's okay with you."

"It's fine with me, Cathy."

She started to stand up and then sat back
again and touched the back of my hand swiftly
and lightly and pulled her fingers away. "Don't
hurt him."

"What?"

"I wouldn't want to think I set anybody onto
him that hurt him. My head knows that he's

an evil man deserving any bad thing that can
happen to him, but my heart says for you not
to hurt him."

"Not unless I have to."

"Try not to have to."

"I can promise that much."

"That's all I wanted." She cocked her head.
"I think maybe you're clever. But he's sly. He's
animal-sly. You know the difference?"

"Yes."

She touched my hand again. "You be
careful."

cuatro

CATHY Kerr sat primly beside me on the genuine leather of old Miss Agnes as we drifted swiftly down through Perrine and Naranja and Florida City, then through Key Largo, Rock Harbor, Tavernier and across another bridge onto Candle Key. Her eagerness to see her child was evident when she pointed out the side road to me and, a hundred yards down the side road, the rock columns marking the entrance to the narrow driveway that led back to the old frame bay-front house. It was of black cypress and hard pine, a sagging weathered old slattern leaning comfortably on her pilings, ready to endure the hurricane winds that would flatten glossier structures.

47

A gang of small brown children came roaring around the corner of a shed and charged us. When they had sorted themselves out, I saw there were but three, all with a tow-headed family resemblance. Cathy kissed and hugged them all strenuously, and showed me which one was Davie. She handed out three red lollipops and they sped away, licking and yelping.

Christine came out of the house. She was darker and heavier than Cathy. She wore faded jeans hacked off above the knee, and a man's white T shirt with a rip in the shoulder. She moved slowly toward us, patting at her hair. She did not carry herself with any of Cathy's lithe dancer's grace, but she was a curiously attractive woman, slow and brooding, with a sensuous and challenging look.

Cathy introduced us. Christine stood there inside her smooth skin, warm and indolent, mildly speculative. It is that flavor exuded by women who have fashioned an earthy and simplified sexual adjustment to their environment, borne their young, achieved an unthinking physical confidence. They are often placidly unkempt, even grubby, taking no interest in the niceties of posture. They have a slow relish for the physical spectrum of food, sun, deep sleep, the needs of children, the caresses of affection. There is a tiny magnificence about them, like the sultry dignity of she-lions.

She kissed her sister, scratched her bare arm, said she was glad to meet me and come on in, there was coffee made recent.

The house was untidy with tracked shell and broken toys, clothing and crumbs. There was a frayed grass rug in the living room, and gigantic Victorian furniture, the dark wood scarred, the upholstery stained and faded. She brought in coffee in white mugs, and it was dark, strong and delicious.

Christy sat on the couch with brown scratched legs curled under her and said, "What I was thinking, that Lauralee Hutz is looking for something, and she could be here days for twenty-five a week and I could maybe make forty-five waitress at the Caribbee, but it would mean getting there and back, and the garden is coming along good, and I got six dollars last week from Gus for crabs, so it don't seem worth it all the way around, getting along the way we are with what you send down, but it's lonely some days nobody to talk with but little kids."

"Did you fix up that tax money?"

"I took it in person, and Mr. Olney he showed me how it figures out a half per cent a month from the time it was first due. I got the receipt out there in the breadbox, Sis."

"Christine, you do how you feel about the job and all."

She gave Cathy a small curious smile. "Max keeps stopping by."

"You were going to run him off."

"I haven't rightly decided," Christine said. She looked me over. "You work at the same place, Mr. McGee?"

"No. I met Cathy through Chookie McCall. I had an errand down this way, so I thought Cathy might like to ride down."

Cathy said abruptly, "Daddy's letters from in the Army, you throw them out going through Ma's things?"

"I don't think I did. What do you want them for?"

"Just to read over again."

"Where they'd be if anyplace, is in the hump-top trunk in that back bedroom, maybe in the top drawer someplace."

Cathy went off. I heard her quick step on the wooden stairs.

"You going around with her?" Christine asked.

"No."

"You married?"

"No."

"She's still legal married to Kerr, but she could say desertion and get loose in six months. A man could do a lot worse. She's strong and she's pretty and she's a worker. She's saddened now, but anybody make her happy, they'd see a different woman. She's a loving one, laughing and singing when she's happy."

"I guess Junior Allen saddened her."

She looked surprised. "You know all about him?"

"Most of it, I guess."

"She must like you to tell you. Cathy is older than me but younger. She doesn't see things about people. I wanted to run him off the place. All that laughing and smiling, and his eyes didn't smile. Then he got to her, loving her up so she couldn't think straight, and it was too late to run him off by then. Even too late to tell her he put his hands on me every chance he had, laughing at me when I called him names. I knew he was after something. I knew he was looking. But I didn't know what for or where it could be. It was a wicked way he did her, Mr. McGee, getting her to need him so bad, then walking out. Better for her if he never come anywhere near here again, but he come back with our money and moved in on a rich woman, and not a damn thing in the world anybody could do about it."

"Go to the police?"

"Police? Whatever he got was already stole one time. Police never did any favors for the Berry family. When you've got a daddy dies in prison, you don't look friendly on the police."

"When was the last time Allen was in the area?"

Suspicion changed her placid face, tightening it. "You wouldn't be some kind of police?"

"No. Absolutely not."

She waited out the fade of suspicion, gave a little nod. "He was coming and going, taking her off on that boat, staying there with her, and maybe a month ago, one day the boat was gone and she was there alone. There's a sale sign on that house and she stays pretty much inside the house and they say she'd turned to drinking more so perhaps Junior Allen is gone for good."

"Perhaps that's just as well, for Cathy's sake."

"He shamed her. People knew what was going on. And they knew Kerr ran out on her. Junior Allen called her names and people heard it. They laugh about her. I clawed one face bone raw and they don't do their laughing in front of me. What Cathy doesn't need is any more trouble. You remember that. I don't think she can take one more little bit of any kind of trouble."

"I don't plan to give her any."

"She looks pretty good now. All slim as a girl." She sighed. "Me, I seem to keep right on widening out."

Cathy came rattling down the stairs with a crushed white box fastened with rubber bands. "They were down in the bottom," she said. "And there was this picture." She showed it to Christine and then brought it over to me. It was a snapshot. A powerful man sat grinning on the top step of the porch of the old house. A placid pretty woman in a print dress sat beside him. The man had his arm around a squinting, towheaded girl of about five. She was leaning against him. A younger girl was in her mother's lap, her fingers in her mouth.

"Old times," Cathy said wistfully. "Suppose

somebody came to us that day and told all of us how things would be. You wonder, would it have changed a thing?"

"I wish that somebody would come along right now," Christine said. "I could use the information. We're due for good luck, Sis. The both of us."

I stood up. "I'll go along and do my errand and stop back for you, Cathy."

"Shall we wait lunch?" Christine asked.

"Better not. I don't know how long I'll be."

The town of Candle Key was a wide place on a fast road. The key was narrow at that point. The town was near the southwest bridge off the key. It had taken a good scouring in 1960 and had a fresh new look, modern gas stations, waterfront motels, restaurants, gift shops, marine supplies, boat yards, post office.

I stopped at the big Esso station and found the station manager at the desk marking an inventory sheet. He was a hunched, seamed, cadaverous man with dusty-looking black hair and his name was Rollo Urthis. He greeted me with the wary regard salesmen grow accustomed to.

"Mr. Urthis, my name is McGee. I'm trying to get a line on the present whereabouts of one Ambrose Allen. Our records show that he worked for you for several months."

"Junior Allen. Sure. He worked here. What's it all about?"

"Just routine." I took a piece of paper from

my wallet, looked at it and put it back.
"There's an unpaid hotel bill of two hundred
and twelve dollars and twenty cents. At the
Bayway Hotel in Miami, back in March. They
put it in the hands of the agency I work for,
and he registered there as coming from Candle
Key."

His grin exposed a very bad set of teeth.
"Now that must be just one of them little
details that Mister Junior Allen overlooked.
When you run acrosst him, he'll probably just
pay you off out of the spare change he carries
in his pocket and give you a big tip for your
trouble, Mister."

"I'm afraid I don't understand, Mr. Urthis."

"He quit me in February and got rich all of a
sudden."

"Did he inherit money?"

"I don't know as that is just the right word.
People got different ideas where he got it. He
was away for nearly a month and came back
on a big cruiser he bought himself, new clothes
and a gold wrist watch no thicker than a silver
dollar. I'd say he made a woman give it to him.
He's the kind can make women do things they
might not want to do if he gave them time to
think about it. He came here and moved right
in with the Berry girls, big as life. Their ma
was still alive then, last year. They had hard
luck, both of them. Cathy is as nice a little
woman as you'd want to know, but he got next
to her pretty quick. When he got the money he
dropped her and moved in on Mrs. Atkinson.

She was a customer a long time, and I could have swore she wouldn't stand for anything like that. But she did. Lost me a customer too. God knows where he's at now. But maybe Mrs. Atkinson would know, if you could get her to talk to you about it. I hear she's touchy on the subject. Nobody around here has seen Junior Allen in better than a month I'd say."

"Was he a satisfactory employee, Mr. Urthis?"

"If he wasn't I wouldn't have kept him. Sure, he was all right. A quick-moving man, real good when we had a rush, and good at fixing things. The trade liked him. He smiled all the time, and he could always find something that needed doing around here. Maybe he was just a little bit too friendly with the women customers, the good-looking ones. Kidding around a little, but nobody complained. Frankly, I was sorry when he quit. The people you get these days, they don't want to work."

"Was he reliable in money matters?"

"I'd say so. I don't think he left owing anybody, and if he did, he sure was able to pay up when he got back. I think he got it off Mrs. Atkinson some way. If so, it would be up to her to complain, not me."

"Where could I find her?"

"See that big real estate sign up the road? Turn right just beyond it and go straight down to the water and turn right again, and it's the second house on the right, a long low white-colored house."

It was one of those Florida houses I find un-sympathetic, all block tile, glass, terrazzo, aluminum. They have a surgical coldness. Each one seems to be merely some complex corridor arrangement, a going-through place, an entrance built to some place of a better warmth and privacy that was never con-structed. When you pause in these rooms, you have the feeling you are waiting. You feel that a door will open and you will be summoned, and horrid things will happen to you before they let you go. You can not mark these houses with any homely flavor of living. When they are emptied after occupancy, they have the look of places where the blood has recently been washed away.

The yard was scrubby with dry weeds. A dirty white Thunderbird rested in the double carport. A new red and white sign in the yard said that Jeff Bocka would be happy to sell this residence to anyone. I stood at the formal entrance, thumbed a plastic button and heard an inside dingle. I heard a faint swift ap-proaching tickety-clack of sandals on tile, and the white door was flung open, and I discarded all preconceived visions of Mrs. Atkinson.

She was a tall and slender woman, possibly in her early thirties. Her skin had the ex-traordinary fineness of grain, and the trans-lucence you see in small children and fashion models. In her fine long hands, delicacy of wrists, floating texture of dark hair, and in the mobility of the long narrow sensitive structuring of her face there was the look of something almost too well made, too highly bred, too finely drawn for all the natural crudities of human existence. Her eyes were large and very dark and tilted and set widely. She wore dark Bermuda shorts and sandals and a crisp blue and white blouse, no jewelry of any kind, a sparing touch of lipstick.

"Who are you? What do you want? Who are you?" Her voice was light and fast and intense and her mouth trembled. She seemed to be on the narrow edge of emotional disaster, holding herself in check with the greatest effort. And about her was a rich and heavy scent of brandy, and an unsteadiness, the eyes too swift and not exactly in focus.

"Mrs. Atkinson, my name is Travis McGee."

"Yes? Yes? What do you want?"

I tried to look disarming. I am pretty good at that. I have one of those useful faces. Tanned American. Bright eyes and white teeth shining amid a broad brown reliable bony visage. The proper folk-hero crinkle at the corners of the eyes, and the bashful appealing smile, when needed. I have been told that when I have been aroused in violent directions I can look like something from an unused corner of hell, but I wouldn't know about that. My mirror consistently reflects that folksy image of the young project engineer who flung the bridge across the river in spite of overwhelming odds, up to and including the poisoned arrow in his heroic shoulder.

So I looked disarming. When they give you something to use, you use it. Many bank robbers look extraordinarily reliable. So you use your face to make faces with, play parts, pick up cues. In every contact with every other human in every day of your life, you become what you sense they want of you or, if you are motivated the other way, exactly what they do not want. Were this not so, there would be no place left to hide.

"I just wanted to talk to you about . . ."

"I won't show the house without an appointment. That was the arrangement. I'm sorry."

They learn that voice and that diction in those little schools they go to before they go on to Smith and Vassar and Wellesley.

"I want to talk to you about Junior Allen."

I could have listed maybe fifty possible reactions without coming close to the one I got. Her eyes dulled and her narrow nostrils flared wide and her mouth fell into sickness. She lost her posture and stood in an ugly way. "That's it, I suppose," she said in a dragging tone. "Certainly. Am I a gift? Or was there a fee?" She whirled and hurried away. She skidded and nearly fell when she turned left at the end of the foyer. I heard an unseen door bang. I stood there in the silence. Then I heard a muffled sound of retching, tiny and far off and agonizing. The noon sun blasted down upon whiteness. I stepped into the relative darkness of the house, into the cool breath of air conditioning. I closed the formal door.

She was still being sick. I went swiftly and quietly through the house. It was as littered as Christine's house, but a different sort of litter. Glasses, dirty ashtrays, food untouched, clothing, things broken in violence. But you could not mark that cold house. In thirty seconds with a fire hose you could have it dripping and absolutely clean. There was no one else there. She was living in this big house like a sick frail animal in a cave.

I could hear water running. I rapped on the closed door.

"Are you all right?"

I heard a murmur I could not interpret. It had a vague sound of reassurance. I roamed around. The place offended me. There was a giant dishwasher in the kitchen. I found a big tray and went through the house collecting the glasses and plates and cups. It took three trips. I scraped stale food into the disposer. Housewife McGee. After I set the dishwasher to churning, I felt a little better.

I went back and listened at the door. There was no sound.

"Are you all right in there?"

The door opened and she came out and leaned against the wall just outside the bathroom door. She had a ghastly pallor and the rings around her eyes looked more smudged.

"Are you moving in?" she asked tonelessly.

"I just came here to . . ."

"This morning I looked at myself, and I

thought maybe the process had to start somewhere, so I got terribly clean. I washed my
hair and scrubbed and scrubbed, and stripped
the bed and even found a drawer with clean
clothing in it, for a wonder. So you're in luck,
aren't you? Excellent timing, provided you
wish to start clean."

"Mrs. Atkinson, I don't think you . . ."

She looked at me with a horrid parody of
sensuality, a sick bright leer. "I suppose you
know all of my specialties, dear."

"Will you listen to me!"

"I'm sure you don't mind if I have a drink
first. I'm really much better after I have some
drinks."

"I've never seen Junior Allen in my life!"

"I hope he told you I've gotten terribly
scrawny and . . ." She stopped the hideous
parody of enticement and stared at me. "What
did you say?"

"I've never seen Junior Allen in my life."

She rubbed her mouth with the back of her
hand. "Why did you come to me?"

"I want to help you."

"Help me what?"

"You said it yourself. The process has to
start somewhere."

"She stared at me without comprehension,
and then with a savage doubt, and finally,
slowly, with belief. She turned, sagging, and,
before I could catch her, she fell to her knees,
bare knees making a painful sound of bone
against terrazzo. She hunched down against

the baseboard and rubbed her face back and forth and began her howling, whooping sobs and coughings. I gathered her up. She shuddered violently at my touch. She was far too light. I took her to her bedroom. When I stretched her out on her freshly made bed, the sobbing stopped abruptly. She became as rigid as dry sticks, her eyes staring at me with glassy enormity, her bloodless lips sucked in. I took her sandals off and covered her with the spread. I fixed the blinds to darken the room, as those helpless eyes followed me. I brought a stool over and put it beside her bed and sat down and took her long frail cold hand and said, "I meant it. What's your name?"

"Lois."

"All right, Lois. Cry. Cry the hell out of it. Rip it all open. Let it go."

"I can't," she whispered. And suddenly she began to cry again. She yanked her hand free, rolled over, rolled her face into the pillow and began the harsh sobbing.

I had to make a guess about what would be right and what would be wrong for her. I had to take a risk. I based the risk on what I know of loneliness, of the need of closeness in loneliness. I stroked her, totally impersonal, the way you soothe a terrified animal. At first she would leap and buck at the slightest touch. After a while there was only a tremor when I touched her, and finally that too was gone. She hiccuped and at last fell down into sleep, curled and spent.

I searched the house until I found her keys. I locked up and left her in the darkened room. I checked the bus schedules and went and got Cathy and took her to where she could catch the bus which would get her home in time. I told her a little of it. There was no question in her mind about my obligation to stay.

cinco

THE doctor's name was Ramirez. He looked like a Swede. He spent a long time with her.

Then he came out and sat at the breakfast bar to drink some of the bad coffee I'd made.

"How is she?"

"Where do you fit in this, McGee?"

"I just stopped to ask her some questions and she fell apart."

He stirred his coffee. "Samaritan, eh?"

"I suppose so."

"Her family should be notified."

"Suppose there isn't any?"

"Then she should be institutionalized. What's the financial situation?"

"I haven't any idea."

"Nice house. Nice car."

"Doctor, what's her condition?"

"Several things. Malnutrition. That plus a degree of saturation with alcohol so she's been having auditory hallucinations. But severe emotional shock is the background for both the other manifestations."

"Prognosis?"

He gave me a shrewd glance. "Fair. A little bit of nerve, a tiny bit of pride, that's all she has left. Keep her tranquilized. Build her up with foods as rich as she can take. Lots of sleep. And keep her away from whomever got her into such a condition."

"A man could do that to a woman?"

"Given a certain type of man and that type of woman, yes. A man like the man who was living with her."

"Did you know him?"

"No. I heard about him. First he was with Catherine Kerr, then with this one. A different social level, eh?"

"Should she talk about Allen?"

"If she's willing to. If she can trust anybody enough, it might be good for her."

"I wonder what happened."

"Things she could not accept. Things she could not live with."

"Not live with?"

"McGee, I do not think it is too dramatic to say you saved her life."

"But she might not trust me."

"Or anyone, ever. That too is a mental disorder. I don't think it's good for her to stay here."

"When can she leave?"

"I will stop by the same time tomorrow. I can tell you then. Give her one of these every four hours. You can stay here?"

"Yes."

"Eggnogs, rich soups, a little at a time, as much as she can hold down. If she gets very agitated, give her one of these. Encourage her to sleep. And talk. Tomorrow we will talk about a nurse. I think she has been physically abused, but I think she has a good constitution."

"Will anybody make any trouble about my staying here?"

"You are adults. You don't look like a fool, McGee. You don't have the look of the kind of murderous fool who'd try to make love to her in her condition. I take you on faith. It saves time. And if anybody does not like this temporary arrangement, I recommended it."

"I'll be too busy with the housework."

"She is exhausted. I think she will sleep a long time now. But it would be nice to be there when she wakes up."

While she was in deep sleep, I collected all the soiled clothing and bedding. I took it into town and dropped it off. I bought supplies. When I got back she was still in almost the same position, making small snores, evenly spaced, barely audible. It took me until dusk to polish the big house. I kept looking in at her.

Then I went in and she made a sound like a whispered scream. She was sitting up. I turned the lights on. Her eyes were huge and vague.

I stayed a cautious ten feet from her and said, "I am Trav McGee. You've been sick. Dr. Ramirez was here. He'll be back tomorrow. I'll stay in the house, so you'll be completely safe."

"I feel so far away. I didn't have any dreams. Unless . . . unless this is one."

"I'm going to go fix you some soup. And bring you a pill."

"I don't want anything."

I arranged more agreeable lighting. She watched me. I had checked where things were kept. I found a sedate nightgown, a robe of Hong Kong silk, tossed them on the foot of the bed.

"If you're strong enough, Lois, get ready for bed while I fix the soup. The bathroom is clean now."

"What is going on? Who are you?"

"Mother McGee. Don't ask questions. Just accept."

I heated the canned soup, strengthened it with cream, fixed her one slice of toast with butter. When I came back she was propped up in bed. She was wearing the nightgown and a bed jacket. She had tied her tousled dark hair back, rubbed away the last trace of lipstick.

"I'm wobbly," she said in a small shy voice.

"Can I have a drink?"

"That depends on how you do with the soup and toast."

"Soup maybe. Toast no."

"Can you feed yourself?"

"Of course."

"Take the pill."

"What is it?"

"Dr. Ramirez called it a mild tranquilizer."

I sat nearby. She spooned the soup up. Her hand trembled. Her nails were clean and broken. There was an old bruise, saffroned, on the side of her slender throat. She was too aware of my watching her and so I tried some mild chatter. Abstract theory by McGee. My tourist theory. Any Ohioan crossing the state line into Florida should be fitted with a metal box that rests against the small of the back. Every ninety seconds a bell rings and a dollar bill emerges part way from a slot in the top of the box. The nearest native removes it. That would take care of the tipping problem. At places where hundreds of them flock together, the ringing of bells would be continuous.

It was difficult to amuse her. She was too close to being broken. The best I could achieve was a very small quick smile. She managed two thirds of the soup and two bites of toast. I set them aside. She slid down a little and yawned.

"My drink?"

"In a little while."

She started to speak. Her eyes blurred and

closed. In a few moments her mouth sagged open and she slept. In sleep the intense strain was gone and she looked younger. I turned the bedroom lights out. An hour later the phone rang. Someone wanted to sell us an attractive building lot at Marathon Heights.

As she slept I searched for the personal data. I finally found the traditional steel box behind books in the living room. It opened readily with a bent paper clip. Birth certificate, marriage license, divorce decree, keys to a safe-deposit box, miscellany of family materials, income statements. I spread it out and pieced together her current status. She had accepted a settlement at the time of divorce three years ago. The house was a part of it. Her income was from a trust account in a bank in Hartford, Connecticut, a family trust setup whereby she received a little over seven hundred dollars a month and could not touch the principal amount. Her maiden name was Fairlea. There was an elder brother in New Haven. D. Harper Fairlea. On her hall table was a great stack of unopened mail. I checked it over and found that people were clamoring to have their bills paid, and in the stack I found her trust income checks, unopened, for May, June and July. Her personal checkbook was in the top drawer of the living-room desk, a built-in affair. She had not balanced it in some time, and I estimated she had a couple of hundred dollars in her account.

At nine-thirty I called D. Harper Fairlea in

New Haven. They said he was ill and could not come to the phone. I asked to talk to his wife. She had a soft, pleasant voice.

"Mr. McGee, surely Lois could tell you that Harp had a severe heart attack some months ago. He's been home a few weeks now, and it is going to be a long haul. Really, I thought the very least she could do was come up here. He is her only blood relative, you know. And I have been wondering why we haven't heard from her. If she is in some sort of trouble and needs help, about all we can say is that we hope things will work out for her. We really can't give her any kind of assistance right now. We have three children in school, Mr. McGee. I don't even want to tell Harp about this. I don't want to give him something else to fret about. I've been inventing imaginary phone calls from Lois, inventing concern and telling him she is fine."

"I'll know better in a few days, how she is and what will have to be done."

"I understood she has some nice friends down there."

"Not lately."

"What is that supposed to mean?"

"I think she gave up her nice friends."

"Please have her phone me when she's able. I'm going to worry about her. But there's just nothing I can do. I can't leave Harp now, and I just don't see how I could take her in."

No help there. She hadn't seemed very concerned about who I might be. I sensed that the

two sisters-in-law had not gotten along too
well. So it was no longer a case of waiting for
somebody to come and take over. I was stuck,
temporarily.

I made up a bed in the bedroom next to hers.
I left my door and her door open. In the middle
of the night I was awakened by the sound of
glass breaking. I pulled my pants on and went
looking. Her bed was empty. The nightgown
and bed jacket were on the floor beside the bed.
The nightgown was ripped.

I found her in the kitchen alcove, fumbling
with the bottles. I turned on the white blaze of
fluorescence and she squinted toward me,
standing naked in spilled liquor and broken
glass. She looked at me but I do not think she
knew me. "Where is Fancha?" she yelled.
"Where is that bitch? I hear her singing."

She was beautifully made, but far too thin.
Her bones were sharp against the smoothness
of her, her ribs visible. Except in the
meagerness of hips and breasts, all the fatty
tissue had been burned away, and her belly
had the slight bloat that indicates starvation. I
got her away from there. Miraculously, she
had not cut her feet. She squirmed with sur-
prising strength, whining, trying to scratch
and bite. I got her back into her bed, and when
she stopped fighting me, I got one of the other
pills down her. Soon it began to take effect. I
put the lights out. I sat by her. She held my
wrist very tightly, and fought against the ef-
fects of the pill. She would start to slide away

and then struggle back to semi-consciousness.
I did not understand a lot of her mumbling.
Sometimes she seemed to be talking to me,
and at other times she was back in her immediate past.

Once, with great clarity, with a mature and
stately indignation she said, "I will not *do*
that!" Moments later she repeated it, but this
time in the lisping narrow voice of a scared
young child. "Oh, I will not *do* that!" The contrast came close to breaking my heart.

And then at last she slept. I cleaned up, hid
the remaining liquor and went back to bed.

In the morning she was rational, and even a
bit hungry. She ate eggs scrambled with butter and cream, and had a slice of toast. She
napped for a little while, and then she wanted
to talk.

"It was such a stupid thing, in the beginning," she said. "You live here all year around,
and you want the natives to like you. You try
to be pleasant. It's a small community, after
all. He was at the gas station. And terribly
cheerful and agreeable. And just a little bit
fresh. If I'd stopped him right in the beginning
... But I'm not very good about that sort of
thing. I guess I've always been shy. I don't like
to complain about people. People who are very
confident, I guess I don't really know how to
handle the situations as they come up. It was
just things he said, and the way he looked at
me, and then one time at the gas station, I had
the top down, he stood by the door on the

driver's side and put his hand on my shoulder.
Nobody could see him doing it. He just held his
hand there and I asked him please not to do
that and he laughed and took his hand away.
Then he got more fresh, after that. But I
hadn't reported him before, and I decided I
would stop trading there, and I did. Then one
day I was at the market and when I came out,
he was sitting in my car and he asked me very
politely if I could drop him off at the station. I
said of course. I expected him to do something.
I didn't know what. And if he did anything, I
was going to stop the car and order him to get
out. After all, it was broad daylight. The moment I got in and shut the door and began to
start the car, he just reached over and . . . put
his hand on me. And he was grinning at me. It
was such . . . such an unthinkable thing, Trav,
so horrible and unexpected that it paralyzed
me. I thought I would faint. People were walking by, but they couldn't see. I couldn't move
or speak, or even think what I should do.
People like me react too violently when they
do react, I guess. I shoved him away and
shouted at him and ordered him out of the car.
He took his time getting out, never stopping
his smile. Then he leaned into the car and said
something about how I'd give him better treat-
ment if he was rich. I told him there was not
that much money in the world. You know,
there is something sickening about that curly
white hair and that brown face and those little
blue eyes. He said that when he made his

fortune he would come back and see how I reacted, something like that, some remark like that."

The orderliness of that portion of the account was an exception. For the rest of it, her mind was less disciplined, her account more random. But it was a good mind. It had insight. Once, as she was getting sleepy, she looked somberly at me and said, "I guess there are a lot of people like me. We react too soon or too late or not at all. We're jumpy people, and we don't seem to belong here. We're victims, maybe. The Junior Allens are so sure of themselves and so sure of us. They know how to use us, how to take us further than we wish before we know what to do about it." She frowned. "And they seem to know by instinct exactly how to trade upon our concealed desire to accept that kind of domination. I wanted to make a life down here, Trav. I was lonely. I was trying to be friendly. I was trying to be a part of something."

Ramirez came in the early afternoon just after I had teased her into eating more than she thought she could. He checked her over.

He said to me, "Not so close to hysteria now. A complex and involved organism, McGee. All physical resource was gone. And just the nerves left, and those about played out. Maybe we can rest them a little now. You wouldn't think it, but there's an awesome vitality there."

I told him of my contact with the family, and

of the wrestling match in the middle of the night.

"She may become agitated again, maybe not so much next time."

"How about a rest home?"

He shrugged. "If you've had enough, yes. But this is better for her. I think she can come back quicker this way. But she can become emotionally dependent upon you, particularly if she learns to talk it out, to you."

"She's been talking."

He stared at me. "Strange you should do all this for her."

"Pity, I guess."

"One of the worst traps of all, McGee."

"What can I expect?"

"I think as she gets further back from the edge she will become placid, listless, somnolent. And dependent."

"You said to get her away from here."

"I'll take a look at her tomorrow."

The thunderheads built high that Thursday afternoon, and after a long hot silence, the winds came and the rain roared down. The sound of the rain terrified her. She could hear, in the sound of the rain, a hundred people all laughing and talking at once, as though a huge cocktail party filled all the other rooms of the sterile house. She became so agitated I had to give her the second one of the quieting pills. She awakened after dark, and she had soaked the sheets and mattress pad with sweat. She said she felt strong enough to take a shower while I changed the bed for her. I had found one last set of clean sheets. I heard her call me, her voice faint. She was crouched on the bathroom floor, wet and naked and sallow as death. I bundled her into a big yellow terry robe and rubbed her warm and dry and got her into bed. Her teeth chattered. I brought her warm milk. It took her a long time to get warm. Her breath had a sour odor of illness. She slept until eleven and then ate a little and then talked some more. She wanted the light out when she talked, and wanted her hand in mine. A closeness. A comfort.

I heard more of it then. A vague outline. She had thought Junior Allen gone forever, and he had come back in the shining cruiser, wearing his brand-new resort clothes, curiously humble and apologetic and anxious for her esteem. He had tied up at her dock, just across the road from the house. She had told him to go away. She kept looking out the windows and saw him sitting disconsolate in his new boat in his new clothes, and at dusk she had gone out onto the dock, endured another profuse apology, then gone aboard for a tour of the cruiser. Once he had her aboard, had her below decks, he was the smiler again, crude and forceful, and he had taken her. She fought him for a long time, but he had been patient. There was no one to hear her. Finally in a kind of terrorized lethargy, she had endured him, knowing he was not quite sane, and thinking this would be the end of it. But it was not. He had kept her aboard with him for two days and two nights, and when he had sensed that she was too dazed and too exhausted and too confused to make even a token resistance, he had moved into the house with her.

"I can't really explain it," she whispered in the darkness. "There was just nothing that had gone before. The only past I knew was him. And he filled the present, and there wasn't any future. I didn't even feel revulsion toward him. Or think of him as a person. He was a force I had to accept. And somehow it began to be terribly important to please him—with the food I cooked for him, the drinks I made for him, the clothes I washed, the continual sex. It was easier to stay a little bit drunk. If I kept him pleased, even that kind of life was endurable. He turned me into an anxious thing, watching him every minute to be certain I was doing what he wanted me to do. I guess that is a kind of physical response to him, not pleasure. A kind of horrid release, a breaking. He learned how to make that happen sometimes, and he'd laugh at me. Then he would go away on that boat and it would be the same, and come back here and it would be the same. I didn't even think of it ever ending. I was too busy getting through each hour as it came along."

She slept then. I went out into the night. The tropical earth was steamy-fresh, bugs chirring and tree toads yelping, and the bay a moony mirror. I sat on the end of her dock and blew smoke at the mosquitoes and wondered why I should be so cynical about her.

It was true that she was a sensitive and introspective woman, and equally true that Junior Allen was a cruel crude bastard, but I could not quite comprehend how his use of her could have brought her to such a state. In the Victorian tradition, it was the fate worse than death, but she was an adult female, and regardless of the method of approach, he had become her lover and had, in time, induced sensuous response in her. I thought of the failure of her marriage and wondered if perhaps she was merely a neurotic headed for breakdown anyway, and Junior Allen had merely hastened the process.

I watched the running lights of a boat heading down the channel, and I heard the grotesque yammering of one of the night birds, and the faraway sobbing of a lovelorn cat.

I went in and checked her in her deep sleep, and went to bed in the neighboring room.

seis

SHE took a good breakfast in the morning and seemed well enough for me to leave her for a time. I went off in Miss Agnes and picked up the laundry and then I made a call on Jeff Bocka, the realtor whose sign stood in Lois Atkinson's yard.

He had a face and head as round and pink as a beach ball. He had that total and almost obscene hairlessness that some diseases cause, a baldness of skull, brows and eyelids. He had amber eyes and small amber teeth.

"Of course I can move that house. I can move it if I can show it, buddy. But I can't show it if that nutty broad screws it up. I made appointments. Twice. What happens? The place is a mess and she is a mess. The first time she is all right for ten minutes, then starts screaming at my clients. The second time she wouldn't even let us in. She's got the place free and clear. There's a recent survey. No cloud on the title. A sound house in a good location. Waterfront. I can move it for forty-five tomorrow, but nobody buys a house if they can't look at it, buddy." He shook his head. "When I get around to it, I take my sign off that lawn."

"When she moves out, if she still wants to sell, I'll leave the keys with you."

"How about the condition of it?"

"It will be okay."

"What do you mean, if she wants to sell?"

"If, on second thought, she's absolutely certain."

"She better move away. She had some friends here. Nice people. Until that gas jockey moved in with her and she started hitting the bottle."

"I guess that offends your sense of morality."

He showed me his little teeth. "This is a decent place."

"They all are, friend."

I walked away and left him standing in the doorway of his cinderblock office, the sunshine making silver highlights on his smooth pink skull.

Ramirez came in the afternoon and marveled at the improvement. She got dressed in the afternoon. She was very reserved. She looked sleepy and moved slowly. In the evening she had another bad spell. And again, in the darkness, she talked.

"I started to come back to life in spite of him, Trav. I seemed to realize that he was trying to destroy me, and I knew I would not be destroyed. I found a little quiet place way back inside myself, and no matter what he made me do, I could go back there and it didn't seem to matter. I began to feel that he had done his worst, and I was in some sense stronger than he was, and I would survive him, and get over him, and get free of him. I began to be able to lift my head and to think of ways of ending it. But . . . he couldn't let that happen, of course. He couldn't let me escape."

It was difficult for her to try to tell me how he had blocked all escape. It became incoherent. And there was much of it she could not remember, fortunately. He kept her drunk so she would be easier to manage, and lessen the chance of her going over the side when she was unguarded.

On that last cruise, Junior Allen had taken the boat over to Bimini. And there he had taken aboard a double-gaited little Haitian slut named Francha, and from there they had gone to a remote bay in the Berry Islands and anchored and stayed there a week, and completed the corruption and destruction of Lois Atkinson. She remembered nothing of the trip back to Candle Key. And there, in June, he had left for good, at his option, knowing he had left that gentle woman with all the explosive images and fragmentary memories that would kill her.

I speculated about motive after Lois had drifted off into sleep. There are men in this world who are compelled to destroy the most fragile and valuable things they can find, the same way rowdy children will ravage a beautiful home. Look at me, they are saying.

Lois, shy, lovely, sensitive, a graceful and cultivated woman, merely by the fact of her existence offered a challenge to Junior Allen. And she had challenged him further by defying him. Even though it meant the stupidity of returning to Candle Key after finding and taking what Sergeant David Berry had hidden, he had to meet that challenge and totally subdue a more delicate morsel than Cathy Kerr could ever be.

The worst crimes of man against woman do not appear on the statues. A smiling man, quick and handy as a cat, webbed with muscle, armored with money, now at liberty in an unsuspecting world, greedy as a weasel in a hen house. I knew the motive. The motive was murder. And this symbolic killing might easily be followed by the more literal act.

Sly and reckless, compulsive and bold. The goat-god, with hoof and smile and hairy ears, satyr at the helm of the *Play Pen*.

Love him, understand him, forgive him, lead him shyly to Freud, or Jesus.

Or else take the contemporarily untenable

position that evil, undiluted by any hint of childhood trauma, does exist in the world, exists for its own precise sake, the pustular bequest from the beast, as inexplicable as Belsen.

I kissed her sweaty temple and tucked the blanket around her narrow shoulder. Symbol of weakness. Symbol of the beast. But I could find no symbol for myself. McGee as avenging angel was a little too much to swallow. I hoped to temper vengeance with greed. Or conversely. Either way, it does simplify the rationalizations.

She began to gorge like a wolf. The anticipated placidity came, bringing small sweet absent smiles, yawns and drowsiness. She dressed and we took walks, and as the edges of bone quickly softened with new flesh, the night talks dwindled. I was in charge of a vegetable woman, mildly amiable, unquestioning, softly remote, an eater and a sleeper, a slow walker. Ramirez was paid off, offering no thoughts for the future. She phoned her sister-in-law, proclaiming that everything was peachy. With me she talked over the segments of a happy childhood. But she did not like the house and did not want the house, or the car. I organized her financial matters, and she signed the deposit slip and all the small checks for the anxious. She wanted to be elsewhere, but did not worry about where, or want the effort of

planning anything. We packed. There was not
much she wanted. Miss Agnes, half truck, ac-
commodated it readily. I took the keys to
Bocka, with the address where she could be
reached. She signed the title and I sold her car,
deposited the cash in her account. She signed
the post office change of address card. I made
the arrangements about the utilities. I took a
last look through the house. She sat out in the
car. I checked all the windows, turned the air
conditioning off, slammed the front door.

As we drove away, she did not look back.
She sat with a dreaming smile, her hands
folded in her lap.

Other people go down to the keys and bring
back shell ashtrays or mounted fish or pottery
flamingos. Travis McGee brings back a Lois Atkinson. The souvenir fervor is the mainstay of
a tourist economy.

"You can stay aboard my houseboat until
you find a place."

"All right."

"Maybe you'd like to go back to New Haven
to be near your brother."

"Maybe I would."

"You should be feeling well enough to travel
pretty soon."

"I guess so."

"Would you rather I found you a place of
your own right away?"

"It doesn't matter."

"Which would you rather do?"

The effort of decision brought her out of torpor. She made fists and her lips tightened. "I guess I have to be with you."

"For a little while."

"I have to be with you."

The patient becomes emotionally dependent upon the analyst. She said it without anxiety. She stated her fact, strangely confident I would accept that fact as completely as she did. In a little while she slumped over against the door and fell asleep. I felt indignant. How could she be so damned certain she had not given herself over into the hands of a Junior Allen of another variety? Where did all this suffocating trust come from? Here was a mature woman who did not seem to know that the wide world is full of monsters, even after one vivid example. I had the feeling that if I told her I was taking her to the cannibal isles to sell her for stew meat, she would wear the same Mona Lisa smile of total acceptance.

I am just not that trustworthy.

Below decks the *Busted Flush* was very hot and very stale and offensively damp. A power failure had kicked the air conditioning off. I had set the thermostat at eighty when I left, minimum power expenditure, just enough to keep it from getting the way it was. I reset it for sixty-five. It would be an hour before it was comfortable. I took her to a place where we could get a good lunch, and brought her back.

She came aboard. I toted her gear aboard. She looked around, mildly and placidly interested. I stowed her and her gear in the other stateroom. She took a shower and went to bed.

I found nine days of mail clogging my box. I weeded it down to a few bills, two personal letters. I phoned Chook. She wanted to know where the hell I'd been. It pleased me that Cathy hadn't told her. I said I'd been staying with a sick friend. She gave me Cathy's number. I phoned her. She sounded very guarded, but said she was alone and told me I could come and see her, and told me how to find it. It was over in town, the top floor of a cheap duplex behind one of the commercial strips along Route One. Pizza, Guaranteed Retreads, Smitty's Sheet Metal, Bonded Warehouse. She lived beyond neon and the wind-whipped fragments of banners announcing forgotten sales.

It was stinking hot upstairs. All buff plaster and ragged wicker, straw and old bamboo. A big fan whizzed and whined by a window, blowing the warm air through. She wore sleazy shorts and a faded halter top. She explained that she shared the place with another dancer from the group and a girl who worked in the local television station. She had two card tables set up. She was stitching away on new costumes for the group. Extra money, she explained. She offered iced tea.

I sat in a wicker chair near the hot breath of the fan and told her about Mrs. Atkinson. Not all of it. She worked and listened. When I leaned back my shirt stuck to the wicker. It had become August while I wasn't looking. She moved around the tables, nipping and stitching, bending and turning, and I was too aware of the modeling of those good sinewy legs, a-gleam with sweat, and the rock-solid roundness of the dancer butt. What I didn't tell her about Lois, she seemed perfectly able to guess. She carried pins in her mouth. The material she worked with was gold and white.

"I thought you'd changed your mind," she said.

"No."

"There's no reason why you shouldn't, Trav." The pins blurred enunciation.

"Were there names and addresses in the letters?"

She straightened. "The ones there were, I put them separate. I can get them for you."

She brought them to me. I read them while she worked. She had a little blue radio turned low, the music merging with the noise of the fan. CMCA, Havana. Voice of the land of peace and freedom and brotherhood. No commercials. Nothing left to sell.

V-Mail, from a long-ago war.

Dear Wife: I have been well and hopping you are the same and the girls too have bought a money order and sending it along later do not try to save all instead buy what you need. I have had a lot of flight time this pass two months but for me it is all cargo work and not dangarous so dont worry about it none. It rains a lot this time of year, more than home even. Since Sugarman got sent elsewhere, we have a new pilot his name is Wm Callowell from Troy New York, a first Lt. and a good safe flyer and he fits in okay with me and George so no worry on that acct. The food isn't much but I am eating good and feeling fine. You tell Cathy I am glad she likes her teacher, and kiss her for me and Christy too and a kiss for yourself as always your loving husb. Dave.

There were other names in other letters. Casual references, less complete. Vern from Kerrville, Texas. Degan from California. I wrote down all the fragments.

She sat with the showgirl brevities in her lap and stitched neatly and quickly. "I didn't know Mrs. Atkinson would be like that," she said thoughtfully.

"It wasn't anything she wanted to get involved in."

"No more'n me. She's beautiful." The brown-eyed look was quick. "You keeping her right there on your boat?"

"Until she feels better."

She crossed the room and put the costumes in a small suitcase and closed the lid. "Maybe she needs help more than I do."

"She needs a different kind of help."

"What are you going to do next?"

"Find out where your father got the money, if I can."

"What time is it?"

"A little after five."

"I've got to change and go out there."

"Have you got a ride?"

"I take a bus mostly."

"I can wait and take you on out."

"I don't like to be a trouble to you, Trav."

I waited. She showered quickly and came out of the bedroom wearing a pink blouse and a white skirt. In moments the blouse was damp and beginning to cling. I drove her on out to Teabolt's Mile O'Beach and went on back to Bahia Mar. My ward had arisen. She had slept so hard her eyes looked puffy, but she had acquainted herself with the equipment in my stainless steel galley, and she wore a pretty cotton dress, which hung just a little loosely on her, and she had taken two generous steaks out of the locker and set them out to thaw. She seemed a little more aware of the situation, shyly aware that she might be a nuisance.

"I could cook and clean and take care of laundry and things like that, and anything else you want me to do, Trav."

"If you feel up to it."

"I don't want to be a dead weight."

"Your job is to get well."

I guess I wasn't particularly gracious. Mine are bachelor ways, tending toward too much order and habit. Some affectionate little guest for a few days is one thing. A party cruise is another. But a lady in residence is potential irritation.

"I can pay my share," she said in a small voice.

"Oh, for God's sake!" I roared. She fled to her stateroom and silently closed the door.

In twenty minutes I felt sufficiently ashamed of myself to look in on her. She was diagonally across the big bed, sound asleep. I made a drink and carried it around until it was gone, and made another, and then went in and shook her awake.

"If you want to cook, it's time to cook."

"All right, Trav."

"Medium rare."

"Yes, dear."

"Don't be so damned humble!"

"I'll try."

After dinner, after she had cleaned up the galley, I brought her into the lounge and asked her if she felt well enough for questions.

"What about?"

"Junior Allen."

Her mouth twisted and she closed her eyes for a moment. She opened them and said, "You can ask questions."

But first I had to brief her. I had to make her understand why I was asking and what I wanted to know. She had heard village gossip about Junior Allen and the sisters. I gave her all of the facts, as I knew them.

For once her new placidity was impaired.

She stared across at me through the lamplight. "He had a lot of cash with him when he came back. I didn't give him anything. So everything, the boat and everything, came from what he took from that place where he was living?"

"That's the only answer."

"But what could it have been?"

"Something he had to go to New York to get rid of."

"Travis, why are you so interested in all this?"

I tried to give her a reassuring smile, but from the look on her face it was not successful. "I am going to take it away from him," I said, in a voice not quite my own.

"I don't understand."

"And keep some of it and give Cathy her share."

"She's important to you?"

"As important as you are."

She thought that over. "Is . . . is this the sort of thing you do?"

"It's in the general area of the sort of thing I do, when I happen to need the money."

"But . . . he seems to be such a dangerous man. And maybe he's spent it all by now. And if he hasn't, how could you get anything away from him? I don't think you could, without killing him."

"I would think of that as a normal business risk, Lois."

The color she had regained drained out of

her face. "How can you say such a terrible
thing? You . . . you've been so good to me."

"What has that got to do with it?"

"But don't you see that . . ."

"I see that you are a damned fool, Lois. You
took me at face value. You decided what sort of
a person I am. If I can't match that image, it
isn't my fault."

After a long silence she said, "Isn't it a
waste?"

"Waste of what?"

"Of *you*! It seems degrading. Forgive me for
saying that. I've seen those African movies.
The lion makes a kill and then clever animals
come in and grab something and run. You're
so bright, Trav, and so intuitive about people.
And you have . . . the gift of tenderness. And
sympathy. You could be almost anything."

"Of course!" I said, springing to my feet and
beginning to pace back and forth through the
lounge. "Why didn't I think of that! Here I am,
wasting the golden years on this lousy barge,
getting all mixed up with lame-duck women
when I could be out there seeking and striving.
Who am I to keep from putting my shoulder to
the wheel? Why am I not thinking about an estate and how to protect it? Gad, woman, I
could be writing a million dollars a year in life
insurance. I should be pulling a big oar in the
flagship of life. Maybe it isn't too late yet! Find
the little woman, and go for the whole bit. Ki-
wanis, P.T.A., fund drives, cookouts, a clean

desk, and vote the straight ticket, yessiree bob. Then when I become a senior citizen, I can look back upon . . ."

I stopped when I heard the small sound she was making. She sat with her head bowed. I went over and put my fingertips under her chin. I tilted her head up and looked down into her streaming eyes.

"Please, don't," she whispered.

"You're beginning to bring out the worst in me, woman."

"It was none of my business."

"I will not dispute you."

"But . . . who did this to you?"

"I'll never know you well enough to try to tell you, Lois."

She tried to smile. "I guess it can't be any plainer than that."

"And I'm not a tragic figure, no matter how hard you try to make me into one. I'm delighted with myself, woman."

"And you wouldn't say it that way if you were."

"Spare me the cute insights."

She shivered and pulled herself together. "I'm grateful to you. I'll try to answer questions."

"What did he say about money?"

She tried. She sat as trim and obedient as a bright girl in class. He said he had all the money he would ever need. Yes, he had repeated that in different ways at different

times. And said he would never have to use
any of it to buy a woman. There was some
hiding place aboard where he kept cash.

"And maybe something else," she said in an
odd voice.

"What?"

"Let me think," she said. Her face was very
still. She had that listening look people wear
when they dig into small vague memories. "A
crooked blue marble," she said. "It was such a
hot day. Sickeningly hot because there was no
wind at all. And all that glare off the water. I'd
drunk too much. I was trying not to be sick.
Their voices were a blur. They were always
arguing about something, shouting at each
other. He was showing her something, and it
fell to the deck, a blue marble, and it rolled
toward her across the teak. It rolled crooked.
She pounced on it and popped it into her
mouth, like a child. I guess she wasn't over
eighteen, but she was as old as all the evil in
the world. He was murderously angry and he
went at her and she ran, laughing at him. He
chased her all over the boat and when he had
her cornered, she dived over the side. She
floated, laughing and squealing at him. She
was naked. She looked very dark in the water,
and I could see her shadow shimmering on the
white sand bottom. He ran and got a gun. It
surprised me that it made such a small snap-
ping noise, but the bullets spit the water up,
close to her, and she came quickly to the
boarding ladder and climbed aboard. He took

her by the nape of the neck and she spat the blue marble into his hand. Then, still holding her, he beat her with his fist until she spent most of the rest of the day down in one of the bunks, whimpering. The marble was a very deep blue. He kept thinking about it and getting mad all over again. He would yell down there, cursing her. He went down once or maybe twice and struck her again." She stared at me with dead eyes and said, "I think I remember it because that was the longest time that they left me alone. Afterwards I kept thinking of the gun. I tried to find it, but I couldn't. When he caught me looking for it, he guessed, and he gave me to her and watched her beat me. She made it look as if she was beating me harder than she was. She wasn't sorry for me. She just didn't want to hurt me so badly I'd be of no use to her. She was terribly hard and chunky and strong. Her legs and thighs were like thick polished mahogany, and she laughed at nothing and she sang all the time in a hard screeching voice, in very bad French. In my empty house, before you came to me, Trav, I kept hearing her singing, as loudly as if she was in the next room."

Some of the old mad light came back into her eyes. "Do you want to hear me sing like Fancha?"

"Take it easy, honey."

"Would you like me to laugh and dance like Fancha?"

She had begun to tremble violently. I hurried to get the pills and brought her one of the strong ones. She didn't try to fight it. She was in bed and asleep in fifteen minutes.

After I had chased the ghastliness of Fancha out of my mind, I settled down to some planning. A trip out to Leavenworth had a deceptive plausibility. It is bad practice to try to question prison people. They live by the book. They need documentation and identification and proper authority. When you can't present it, they immediately wonder if you are there to try to help somebody slip out. I decided that was the last resort. I would chase down every other lead, and if they all dwindled to absolutely nothing, then I would go out there to Kansas and get the feel of it and try to con somebody.

Before I went to bed, I took a look at my ward. In the faint light she looked no more than nineteen, gentle, and unmarked by any ugliness.

siete

IN the morning I tried the William Callowells of Troy, New York.

Such chances run small. If he lasted out that war, and stayed out of a police action, and avoided civil disaster, maybe he could be a roamer, that address gone stale in a transient world.

Troy had a pair of them. William B. William M. The efficient operator took the numbers of both from Troy information, and I tried it by the alphabet. William B.'s home gave us another number. A girl said it was Double A Plastics, and three minutes later I had the wary voice of William B. A pilot in World War

Two? Hell, no, he was twenty-six years old, and a chemical engineer and he had lived in Troy less than a year and knew there was another Wm. in the book, but knew nothing about him. Thanks so much. You are entirely welcome.

My LDO left the circuit open and I heard a woman answer the William M. number. She had a small unsteady voice. She responded in a very formal manner. "I regret to say that Mr. Callowell passed away last March."

I asked to speak to her. "Mrs. Callowell, I am sorry to hear about your husband."

"It was a blessing. I prayed for his release."

"I just wonder if he was the Mr. Callowell I'm trying to locate. Was he a pilot in World War Two?"

"My goodness no! You must mean my son. My husband was eighty-three years of age."

"Can I get in touch with your son, Mrs. Callowell?"

"Why, if you had called yesterday you could have talked to him. We had a wonderful visit."

"Where can I reach him?"

"The operator said you are calling from Florida. Is it terribly urgent?"

"I would like to reach him."

"Just a moment. I have it written down here. His home, of course, is in Richmond, Virginia. Let me see. Today is the . . . third, isn't it. He will be at the convention in New York City through Tuesday the ninth. At the Americana Hotel. I suppose you could reach

him there, but he said there would be a great
many meetings and he would be very busy."

"Thank you so much, Mrs. Callowell. By the
way, where was your son's overseas duty?"

"In India. He has always wanted to go back
and see the country again. He wrote such
wonderful letters from there. I saved them all.
Maybe one day he will have the chance."

I hung up and finished my half cup of tepid
coffee. I phoned an airline. They had one at the
right time. Idlewild by 2:50 p.m. Lois seemed
very disconcerted at the prospect of being left
alone. She looked as if her teeth might chatter.
Her eyes were enormous. I instructed her as I
packed, and made her write down the briefing.
Mail, laundry, phone, groceries, the manual
switch to kick the air conditioner back on, gar-
bage disposal, reliable local doctor, how to lock
up, etc., television channels, cozy bookshelf,
fire extinguishers, and a few small items of
standard marine maintenance. She bit a pale
lip and scribbled it all. She needed neither car
nor bike. Everything, including the public
beach, was walkable. Take the white pills
every four hours. Take a pink one if you start
to shake apart.

At the gangplank I kissed her like any com-
mutation ticket husband, told her to take care
of herself, scuttled toward Miss Agnes, slap-
ping my hip pocket where the money and the
credit cards were. The unemployed merit no
credit cards. But I had a guarantor, a man for
whom I had done a sticky and dangerous favor, a

man whose name makes bank presidents spring to attention and hold their shallow breaths. The cards are handy, but I hate to use them. I always feel like a Thoreau armored with a Leica and a bird book. They are the little fingers of reality, reaching for your throat. A man with a credit ard is in hock to his own image of himself.

But these are the last remaining years of choice. In the stainless nurseries of the future, the feds will work their way through all the squalling pinkness tattooing a combination tax number and credit number on one wrist, followed closely by the I.T. and T. team putting the permanent phone number, visaphone doubtless, on the other wrist. Die and your number goes back in the bank. It will be the first provable immortality the world has ever known.

Manhattan in August is a replay of the Great Plague of London. The dwindled throng of the afflicted shuffle the furnace streets, mouths sagging, waiting to keel over. Those still healthy duck from one air-conditioned oasis to the next, spending a minimum time exposed to the rain of black death outside.

By five minutes of four I was checked into the hotel. They had a lot of room. They had three conventions going and they still had a lot of room. Once inside the hotel, I was right back in Miami. Same scent to the chilled air, same skeptical servility, same glorious decor—as if a Brazilian architect had mated an air terminal with a manufacturer of cotton padding. Lighting, dramatic. At any moment the star of the show will step back from one of the eight (8) bars and break into song and the girlies will come prancing in. Keep those knees high, kids. Keep laughing.

Wm. M. Callowell, Jr., was not listed under his own name, but under the Hopkins-Callowell, Inc. suite, 1012-1018. I asked the desk which convention that was. "Construction," he said. "Like they make roads."

A man in the suite answered the phone with a young, hushed and earnest voice, and said he would check Mr. Callowell's agenda. He came back in a moment and said in an even more hushed voice, "Sir, he just this moment returned from a meeting. He's having a drink here now, sir."

"Will he be there long?"

"I would imagine at least a half hour."

I checked myself in a full-length mirror. I smiled at Mr. Travis McGee. A very deep tan is a tricky thing. If the clothing is the least bit too sharp, you look like an out-of-season ball player selling twenty pay life. If it is too continental, you look like a kept ski instructor. My summer city suit was Rotarian conservative, dark, nine-ounce orlon looking somewhat but not too much like silk. Conservative collar on the white shirt. Rep tie. A gloss on the shoes. Get out there and sell.

Gleam those teeth. Look them square in the eye. You get out of it what you put into it. A smile will take you a long way. Shake hands as if you meant it. Remember names.

There were a dozen men in the big room. They had big voices and big laughs and big cigars and big glasses of whisky. Junior executives were tending bar for them, sidling in to laugh at the right time, not too loudly, at all evidences of wit. They wore no badges. That is the key to the small and important convention. No badges, no funny hats. Any speakers they get are nationally known. And they order their food off the full menu.

One of the juniors told me that Mr. Callowell was the one over there by the big windows, with the glasses and mustache. William Callowell was in his middle forties. Average size. Somewhat portly. It was difficult to see what he looked like. He had a stand-up ruff of dense black hair, big glasses with black frames, a black mustache, and he smoked a big black pipe. There didn't seem to be enough skin showing. The only thing unchangeably his was a wide fleshy nose with a visible pattern of pores. He was talking with two other men. They stopped abruptly when I was six feet away and they all stared at me.

"Excuse me," I said. "Mr. Callowell, when it's convenient I'd like a word with you."

"You one of the new Bureau people?" one of his friends asked.

"No. My name is McGee. It's a personal matter."

"If it's that opening, this isn't the time or the place, McGee," Callowell said in a soft unfriendly voice.

"Opening? I gave up working for other people when I was twenty years old. I'll wait in the hall, Mr. Callowell."

I knew that would bring him out fast. They have to know where you fit. They have those shrewd managerial eyes, and they can look at a man and generally guess his salary within ten per cent either way. It is a survival reaction. They're planted high on the side of the hill, and they want to know what's coming up at them, and how fast.

He came lounging out, thumbing a new load into his pipe.

"Personal matter?"

"I came up from Florida this afternoon just to see you."

"You could have phoned and I would have told you I have too heavy a load here."

"This won't take much time. Do you remember a crew chief named Sergeant David Berry?"

It snapped him way back into the past. It changed his eyes and the set of his shoulders. "Berry! I remember him. How is he?"

"He died in prison two years ago."

"I didn't know that. I didn't know anything about that. Why was he in prison?"

"For killing an officer in San Francisco in nineteen forty-five."

"Good Lord! But what's that got to do with me?"

"I'm trying to help his daughters. They need help."

"Are you an attorney, Mr. McGee?"

"No."

"Are you asking me to help Berry's daughters financially?"

"No. I need more information about David Berry."

"I didn't know him very well or very long."

"Anything you can tell me will be helpful."

He shook his head. "It was a long time ago. I can't take the time right now." He looked at his watch. "Can you come back at eleven?"

"I'm registered here."

"That's better. I'll come to your room as near eleven as I can make it."

"Room seventeen-twenty, Mr. Callowell."

He rapped on my door at eleven-twenty. He'd had a full measure of good bourbon and a fine dinner and probably some excellent brandy. It had dulled his mind slightly, and he was aware of that dullness and was consequently more careful and more suspicious than he would have been sober. He refused a drink. He lowered himself into a comfortable chair and took his time lighting his pipe.

"I didn't catch what you do for a living, Mr. McGee."

"I'm retired."

He hoisted one black eyebrow. "You're young for that."

"I keep myself busy with little projects."

"Like this one?"

"Yes."

"I think I better know a little more about this project."

"Let's lay down the shovels, Mr. Callowell. I'm not on the make for anything you have. Berry came home rich from his little war. I'd like to find out how. And if I can find out how, maybe I can get a little of it back for his girls. His wife is dead. All this will cost you is a little time. And a little remembering."

For a little while I thought he had gone to sleep on me. He stirred and sighed. "There were ways to get rich over there. They said it was even better earlier in the war. Berry had been there a long time before I came along. ATC. Flying C-46's out of Chabua in Assam. Passengers and cargo. Calcutta, New Delhi, and over the Hump to Kunming. Go sometimes to twenty-two thousand feet in those creaking laboring bastards, and then come down through the ice and get your one and only pass to lay it down at Kunming. I'd say I made twenty-five flights with Berry. No more. I didn't get to know him. Crews didn't stay together too long in that deal. The first one I had, my first airplane over there, quit.

Structural failure, and the landing gear collapsed, and I slid it a long long way. Just three in a crew. They split us up. I got the ship Berry was on. Berry and George Brell, copilot. I was uneasy, wondering if Brell thought he should have been moved up. Their pilot wangled a transfer out."

"Sugarman?"

"That was the name! He was killed later. Brell didn't resent me. It worked out all right. Brell and Berry were competent. But they weren't friendly. Berry was pretty surly and silent, but he knew his job. I think he was sort of a loner. We had probably twenty-five flights together, probably ten of those round trips to China. Then one night we came up from Calcutta and I had let down to about a thousand feet when the starboard engine caught fire without any warning at all. It really went. Too much for the extinguisher system. I goosed it up to as much altitude as I dared, leveled it off and we went out one two three. Five seconds after my chute opened, the wing burned off and it went in like a rock, and five seconds after that I landed in a bed of flowers right in front of the station hospital and wrenched my ankle and knee. Very handy indeed. I hobbled in with my arm around a great big nurse. Berry and Brell visited me and thanked me and brought me a bottle, and I never saw them again."

"Did you hear any rumors about Berry making money?"

"I seem to remember hearing a few vague things. He was the type. Very tough and silent and cute."

"How would he have done it?"

"By then the most obvious way was by smuggling gold. You could buy it in Calcutta, and sell it on the black market in Kunming for better than one and a half times what you paid for it. And get American dollars in return. Or, take Indian rupees and bring them back and convert them into dollars at Lloyd's Bank. Or buy the gold with the rupees. It could be pretty flexible. But they were cracking down on it. It was a risk I didn't want to take. And I knew that if Berry or Brell was doing it, and got caught, there would be a cloud on me. So I kept my eyes open. You could do a lot with gold in China then. They had that runaway inflation going, and damn few ways to get the gold in there. You could even make a profit by smuggling rupee notes in large denominations into China. They say the Chinese used the rupees to trade with the Japs. The Japs liked the rupees to finance their espionage in India. Hell, the Chinese were trading pack animals to the Japs in return for salt. It was a busy little war. I think Berry was a trader. He had that native shrewdness. And I think he had the knack of manipulating people. Once I think he actually sounded me out, but there was nothing I could put my finger on. I must have given him the wrong answers."

"Was he close to George Brell?"

"Let's say a little closer than a sergeant and a lieutenant usually get, even in an air crew. They were together quite a while."

"Then Brell, if still living, is the next man to talk to."

"I know where you can find him."

"Really!"

He hesitated. It was the business syndrome. He had something somebody else wanted and he had to stop for a moment to consider what advantage might be gained. This reflex brought him all the way back from the jungly old war in the back alcove of memory, where he was Lieutenant Callowell, agile, quick and very concerned about the ways of hiding and controlling the fear he felt every day. He felt back into the portly disguise of William M. Callowell, cushioned with money and authority, shrewd builder and bidder, perhaps privately worried about impotence, audits and heart attacks. I could sense he did not often think of the war. There are middle-aged children who spend a part of every day thinking of their college or their war, but the ones who grow up to be men do not have this plaintive need for a flavor of past importance, and Callowell was one of these.

He relit his pipe, shifted his weight. "Two years ago there was a short article in *Newsweek* about our operation, in connection with the Interstate program. They used my picture. I got letters from people I hadn't heard from in years. Brell wrote me from Harlingen, Texas, sounding like a dear old flyboy buddy, which he wasn't. Letterhead stationery, thick parchment bond, tricky type-face. Brell Enterprises I think it was. One inch of congratulations to me, and a yard of crap about how well he was doing, closing with the hope we could get together and talk over old times. I answered it with a very short cool note, and I've heard nothing since."

"You didn't like the man."

"For no reason I can put my finger on, McGee. We had dull, dirty, dangerous duty over there, but, after all, it was Air Transport Command. Brell was the tailored uniform type, with the hundred mission cap, and when we were in Calcutta he'd put on the right hardware and turn himself into a Flying Tiger and cut one hell of a swath through the adoring lassies. And he toted a thirty-eight with pearl grips instead of the regulation forty-five. And he didn't like to make landings. He would get very sweaty and overcontrol when he made landings."

"He would have the information on David Berry, then."

"If he's willing to talk. If he was in on it, on any cute money on the side, why should he talk to anybody about it?"

"I've leveled with you, Mr. Callowell, but I might try something else with Brell."

"And use my name in vain, McGee?"

"It might occur to me."

"I would advise against it. We have lawyers without enough to do. They get restless."

"I'll bear that in mind."

"I don't often do this much talking for so little reason, McGee. You have a nice touch. You're an eager listener. You smile in the right places. It puts people on. And, of course, you haven't leveled with me."

"How can you say such a thing!"

He chuckled and pulled himself to his feet. "End of session, McGee. Good night and good luck." At the door he turned and said, "I'll have you checked out, of course. Just for the hell of it. I'm a careful and inquisitive man."

"Can I make it easier by giving you my address?"

He winked. "Slip F-18. Bahia Mar. Lauderdale."

"Mr. Callowell, I am impressed."

"Mr. McGee, any reasonably honest man in the construction industry either sets up his own CIA or he goes broke." He chuckled again and trudged toward the elevators, trailing fragrant smoke.

ocho

In the morning I placed a station call to the number listed for George Brell in Harlingen. I got a lazy-toned switchboard operator who put me through to a sharp-voiced secretary who said that Mr. Brell was not in his office yet. As she had no way of knowing it was a long distance call, I side-stepped her request for my name and said I would phone later.

Then I phoned my barge boat. After three rings, I heard her voice, small, tense, cautious. "Hello?"

"This is your night nurse speaking."

"Trav! Thank God."

"What's the matter? Is something wrong?"

"Nothing in particular. Just . . . I don't know

111

. . . tension, I guess. I got so used to you being nearby. I hear sounds. And I jump. And I had bad dreams."

"Cook them out in the sun."

"I'm going to. On the beach, maybe. When are you coming back?"

"I'm going to Texas today."

"What?"

"There's a man there I want to see. I might be back there by Friday, but I'm not certain. Take your pills, honey. Don't agitate yourself. Eat, sleep and keep busy. You're smack in the middle of hundreds of boats and thousands of people."

"Trav, a woman phoned and she's very anxious to get in touch with you. She said it's an emergency. It sort of put her off stride to have a woman answer and say you're away. I said you might phone and she said to tell you to phone her. Miss McCall. With a very strange first name. I don't know if I have it right."

"Chookie."

"That's it."

I had her look in my book and give me the number. By the time I hung up, Lois sounded pretty good. I wondered if I had been a damn fool not to lock up my liquor supply, or at least to arrange to have somebody stay with her. Hurry home, Mother McGee. People have their acquired armor, made up of gestures and expressions and defensive chatter. Lois's had all been brutally stripped away, and I knew her as well as anybody ever had or ever would. I knew her from filled teeth to the childhood apple tree, from appendix scar to wedding night, and it was time for her to start growing her new carapace, with me on the outside. I caught her raw, and did not care to be joined to her by scar tissue when healing began.

Chook's phone went to nine rings before she answered in the gritty rancor of interrupted sleep. But her voice changed when she recognized mine. "Trav! I phoned you last night. Who is that Mrs. Atkinson?"

"One of your more successful rivals."

"I mean really. Is she the one that whosis took on when he dropped Cathy?"

"Yes."

"Trav, I phoned about Cathy. She worked the first show last night. She seemed fine. And then they found her unconscious out on the beach there at the hotel. She'd been terribly beaten. Her face is a mess. Two broken fingers. They don't know yet if there's any internal injuries. She regained consciousness before they got her to the hospital. The police questioned her. She told them she went out to walk on the beach and somebody jumped her and beat her up. She couldn't give them a description. I talked to her next, after they'd given her a sedative. She acted very strange about it. I think it was him, Trav. She won't be able to work for two weeks anyway, maybe longer. She's really a mess."

"Does she want to talk to me?"

"She doesn't want to talk to anybody. It's in

the paper today. Show girl assaulted on private beach. Mysterious assailant and so on."

"Are you going to see her today?"

"Of course!"

"I might not get back before Saturday. Look in on Lois Atkinson if you get a chance. Our friend left her in pretty sad shape. She's a lady."

"Oh, rally?"

"With ragged edges. You'll like her, I think. Make girl talk. Then I'll try to phone you tonight at the hotel, for a report on both of them."

"McGee's clinic?"

"The Junior Allen discard club. Take care."

A travel office at the hotel helped me find the best way to get to the Rio Grande Valley. A direct 707 out of Idlewild to Houston, a two-hour layover and then a feeder flight down to Harlingen with one stop at Corpus Christi. I had barely missed a better deal, and so I could take my time getting out to Idlewild.

The flight took off with less than half the seats occupied. The whole country lay misty-bright, impersonal, under a summer high, and we went with the sun, making noon last a long time. The worst thing about having a hundred and eighty million people is looking down and seeing how much room there is for more. A stewardess took a special and personal interest in me. She was a little bigger than they usually are, and a little older than the norm. She was styled for abundant lactation, and her uniform blouse was not. She had a big white smile and she was mildly bovine, and I had the curious feeling I had met her before, and then I remembered where—in that valuable book by Mark Harris, *Bang the Drum Slowly*, the stewardess that "Author" runs into when he is on his way out to Mayo's. My stewardess perched on the edge of the seat beside me, back arched, smiling.

"Houston is going to be wicked hot," she said. "I am going to get me into that motel pool as fast as I can, and come out just long enough every once in a while to get a tall cold drink. Some of the kids just stay in the rooms, but I think they keep them too cold. It gives me the sinus. I layover there and go out at ten tomorrow, and somehow Houston is always a drag, you know?"

The mild misty blue eyes watched me and the mouth smiled and she waited for my move. You can run into the Tiger's Perpetual Floating House Party almost anywhere. At 28,000 feet, and at the same 800 fps muzzle velocity of a .45 caliber service pistol. Nobody leaves marks on anybody. You meet indirectly, cling for a moment and glance off. Then she would be that hostess in Houston and I would be that tanned one from Florida, a small memory of chlorinated pool water, fruit juice and gin, steak raw in the middle, and hearty rhythms in the draperied twilight of the tomb-cool motel cubicle, riding the grounded flesh of the jet-stream Valkyrie. A harmless pleasure. For harmless plastic people, scruff-proof, who can create the delusion of romance.

But it is a common rudeness to refuse the appetizer without at least saying it looks delicious.

"I'd settle for Houston," I said with a manufactured wistfulness. "But I'm ticketed through to Harlingen."

The smile did not change and the eyes became slightly absent. She made some small talk and then swayed down the aisle, smiling, offering official services. Most of them find husbands, and some of them are burst or burned in lonely fields, and some of them become compulsively, forlornly promiscuous, sky sailors between the men in every port, victims of rapid transit, each flight merely a long arc from bed to bed.

I saw her later in the Houston terminal, stilting along, laughing and chattering into the face of a big florid youngster in a nine-gallon hat.

I was in Harlingen at a little after five, the sun high and blazing, the heat as wet and thick as Florida's. I rented an air-conditioned Galaxie and found a tall glassy motel with green lawns, pool and fountains, and checked into a shadowed icy room facing the pool. I showered and changed to sport shirt and slacks. I drove around. It was a village trying to call itself a city. Pale tall buildings had been put up in unlikely places for obscure reasons. It was linked to Brownsville by the twenty-five mile umbilicus of Route 77. The George Brell residence was at 18 Linden Way, Wentwood. Big plots, big sweeping curves of asphalt. Architectured houses, overhangs, patios, sprinklers, driveways and turnarounds pebbled in brown, traveler palms, pepper trees, Mexican gardeners, housewives in shorts, antique wrought-iron name signs. Number eighteen was blonde stone, glass, redwood, slate. Formal plantings. A black Lincoln and a white Triumph in the drive, a black poodle in a window of the house, glaring out at the world.

I went back among the common people and found a beer joint. Standard opening conversation gambit. "Sure hot." Standard answer. "Sure is."

The beer was so cold it had no taste. The juke played hill country laments. I found a talkative salesman. Local economy: Damned town had been too long at the mercy of the Air Force. Close the base, open the base, et cetera. Oranges and grapefruit were basic. Bad freeze year and everything goes to hell. Little winter tourist business building up pretty good. Padre Island and so forth. More transient traffic through into Mexico now the Mexicans fixed their damn road decent from Matamoros to Victoria. Quickest way from the States to Mexico City. He was talkative and cranky.

I got him onto local success stories, and

when he got onto George Brell I kept him
there. "Old George is into a lot of things. His
wife had some groves, and now he's got more.
His first wife, dead now. God knows how many
of those Beeg-Burger drive-ins he's got now. A
dozen. More. And the real estate business, and
warehouse properties, and the little trucking
business he's started up."

"He must be a smart man."

"Well, let's say George is a busy man. He
keeps moving. They say he's always in some
kind of tax trouble, and he couldn't raise a
thousand dollars cash, but he lives big. And he
talks big. He likes a lot of people around him
all the time."

"You said he married again?"

"Few years back. Hell of a good-looking girl,
but I don't think she's more than maybe three
years older than his oldest girl from his first
wife. Built her a showplace house out in Wentwood Estates. Gerry, her name is."

My salesman had to get on home, and after
he had gone I went back to a booth and phoned
George Brell. It was ten to seven. I got him on
the line. He sounded emphatic. I said I wanted
to see him on a personal matter. He became
wary. I said that Bill Callowell had suggested
he might be able to help me.

"Callowell? My old pilot? Mr. McGee, you
come right on out to the house right now.
We're just sitting around drinking, and we'll
have one ready for you."

I drove out. There were a half-dozen cars

there. A house man let me in. Brell came hurrying to me to pump my hand. He was a
trim-bodied man in his late forties, dark and
handsome in a slightly vulpine way, and I suspected he wore a very expensive and in-
conspicuous hair piece. He looked the type to
go bald early. He had a resonant voice and a
slightly theatrical presence. He wore tailored
twill ranch pants and a crisp white shirt with
blue piping. Within ten seconds we were Trav
and George, and then he took me out to a
glassed back deck where the people were. A
dozen of them, seven men and five women,
casually dressed, friendly, slightly high. As he
made the introductions he managed to give me
the impression that all the men worked for
him and he was making them rich, and all the
women were in love with him. And he made it
known to them that I was a dear friend of one
of the most influential road builders in the
country, a man who had flown desperate mis-
sions with George Brell, and had survived only
because George was along. His wife, Gerry,
was a truly stunning blonde in her middle
twenties, tall and gracious, but with eyes just
a little cold to match a smile so warm and wel-
coming.

We sat around on the sling chairs and
leather stools, and talked the dusk into night.
Two batches left, cutting the group down to
five. They made it unthinkable not to stay to
dinner. The Brells, a young couple named
Hingdon and me. A little while before dinner,

Brell took Hingdon off to discuss some business matter with him. Mrs. Hingdon went to the bathroom. Gerry Brell excused herself and went to see how the preparation of dinner was coming.

I went wandering. A harmless diversion. It was a big rambling house, obviously furnished by a decorator who had worked with the architect. And they had not been in it long enough to add those touches that would spoil the effect. There was a room off the living room, a small room with lights on inside. I saw a painting on the far wall of the small room that looked interesting. I listened and there was no sound of voices from the small room. I thought Hingdon and Brell might have gone in there. So I wandered in for a closer look at the painting. Just as I reached the middle of the room I heard a gasp and a scuffling noise. I turned and saw there were two people on a deep low couch to the right of the doorway. The couch had high sides, and I had not noticed them.

One was a pale-haired girl of about seventeen. She was slumped back in the couch against pillows. She had on short khaki shorts and a pale gray blouse unbuttoned to the waist. She had the long sprawled luxurious body of maturity, and she was breathing deeply, her face revealing that telltale slackness, the emptiness of prolonged sexual excitement. It was a child's mouth and a child's eyes set into a woman's face. Her lips were wet and her nipples swollen, and she was very slow in coming back from the dreamy land of eros. The boy was older, twenty possibly, and he was a massive brute, all hair and muscles and jaw corners and narrow infuriated eyes.

Left to my own devices, I would have gone very quietly away from there. But her warrior gave me no chance. "Why don't you knock, you silly son of a bitch?" he said in a gravelly voice.

"I didn't know it was a bedroom, boy."

He stood up, impressively tall and broad. "You insulted the lady."

The lady was sitting erect, buttoning her blouse. The lady said, "Deck him, Lew!" Sick him, Rover. He swarmed at me, obedient as any dog.

I am tall, and I gangle. I look like a loose-jointed, clumsy hundred and eighty. The man who takes a better look at the size of my wrists can make a more accurate guess. When I get up to two twelve I get nervous and hack it back on down to two oh five. As far as clumsiness and reflexes go, I have never had to use a flyswatter in my life. My combat expression is one of apologetic anxiety. I like them confident. My stance is mostly composed of elbows.

Lew, faithful dog, wanted it over right now. He hooked with both hands, chin on his chest, snorting, starting the hooks way back, left right left right. He had fists like stones and they hurt. They hurt my elbows and forearms and shoulders, and one glanced off the top of my shoulder and hit me high on the head. When I had the rhythm gauged, I counter punched and knocked his mouth open with an overhand right. His arms stopped churning and began to float. I clacked his mouth shut with a very short left hook. He lowered his arms. I put the right hand in the same place as before and he fell with his mouth open and his eyes rolled up out of sight.

The little lady screamed. People came running. I massaged my right hand. "What's going on!" Brell yelled. "What the hell is going on!"

I was too angry for polite usage, for the living room turn of phrase. "I walked in here to look at the painting. I thought the room was empty. This crotch jockey had his little girl all turned on and steaming and they resented the interruption, and she told him to deck me. But it didn't work out."

Brell turned on the girl, anguish in his voice. "Angie! Is this true?"

She looked at Lew. She looked at me. She looked at her father. Her eyes were like stones. "What do you really care *who* gets laid around here *anyway!*" She sobbed and brushed by him and fled. After a stunned hesitation, he ran after her, calling to her. A door slammed. He was still yelling. A sports car rumbled and snorted and took off. Rubber yelped. It faded, shifting up through the gears.

"God love us," Gerry Brell said. She took a

vase from the table and stood thoughtfully and dumped it on Lew's head, flowers and all. The Hingdons and I were busy trying not to look squarely at one another.

Lew pushed the floor away and sat up. He looked like a fat sad baby. His eyes were not properly focused.

Gerry sat on her heels beside him and put her hand on that meaty shoulder and shook him gently. "Sweetie, you better haul your ass out of here right now, because if I know George Brell, he's loading a gun right this minute."

The eyes focused, comprehended, became round and wide with alarm. He jumped up and without a glance at anyone or another word went running heavily and unsteadily out.

Gerry smiled at us and said, "Excuse me, please." She went off to find George.

Little Bess Hingdon stayed close to her big and rather solemn young husband as we went into the long living room. "Dear, I really think we should go."

"Just leave?" Hingdon said uncertainly.

There was a nice flavor about them, that scent of good marriage. Separated by a room of people, they were still paired, still aware of each other.

"I'll find Gerry," she said and went off.

Sam Hingdon looked curiously at me and said, "That Lew Dagg is a rough boy. Linebacker. One more year to go, and the pros are watching him."

"Like what did I hit him with?"

He grinned. "Something like that."

"Maybe he's out of condition. He should use the summer for a different kind of exercise. Is that Angie George's eldest?"

"Youngest. She's the only one left home. Gidge is the eldest. She's married to a boy in med school in New Orleans. Tommy's in the Air Force. They're Martha's children."

Bess came hurrying in, carrying her purse. "It's all right, honey. We can leave now. Good night, Mr. McGee. Hope we'll see you again."

I went out to the terrace and made myself a weak drink. I could hear Gerry and George yammering at each other. I could hear the music but not the lyrics. Fury and accusation. A pretty girl in dark braids and a uniform came onto the terrace and gathered up the debris of the cocktail snacks, gave me a shy glance and cat-footed away.

Finally George came out. He looked sour. He grunted at me, poured bourbon over one cube and downed it before the ice had a chance to chill it. He banged the glass down. "Trav, Gerry has a headache. She said to apologize. Jesus, what an evening!"

"Apologize to her for me. Tell her I didn't stop to think that could be your daughter when I spoke so rough. I was still angry. And about hitting that kid, he gave me no choice."

He stared at me with evident agony. "Just what were they doing, McGee?"

"I didn't actually see them doing anything. He had her blouse unbuttoned and her bra un-hooked, but she had her shorts on."

"She doesn't even start college until fall. Goddamn that ape! Let's get out of here, Trav."

We went out and got into the Lincoln. He drove swiftly through a long maze of curving roads and then slowed as we passed a house as conspicuous as his. I caught a glimpse of the Triumph. He speeded up. "Gerry said that's where she'd go. It's her closest girl friend."

He didn't speak again until we were on 77 heading south. "It's a hell of a thing for something like that to happen, the first time you're in my home."

"Worse for you than for me."

"How the hell am I supposed to keep an eye on her? That's Gerry's job and she's goofing it. She says she can't control her. She says Angie won't listen to her. I'm a busy man, goddamn it. I've got to send the kid away, but where? Where can you send them in August, for God's sake? There's no relatives to park her with. Did you hear what she said to me?" He banged the steering wheel with the heel of his hand. "What do you think, McGee? Do you think that ape is actually screwing my little girl?"

"I think you're driving too damned fast, George. And I don't think he is. Yet."

"Sorry. Why don't you think he is?"

"Because if he was, he would have had her off someplace where he could, without interruption. And from the look of her, that was the next step, George."

He slowed down a little more. "You know, that makes sense. Sure. He's probably trying to talk her into it. He's been hanging around for about a month. Trav, that's the second good turn you've done me tonight."

"And she doesn't care too much for the boy."

"How do you know?"

"When she ran out, he hadn't moved a muscle. She couldn't know but what I'd killed him."

"That's right! I'm feeling better by the minute. McGee, you must have a very nice punch."

"He's very easy to hit. And you're going too fast again."

We came into Brownsville. He took a confusing number of turns and put the car in a small lot on a back street. We walked half a block through the sultry night to the shabby entrance of a small private club, a men's club, with a comfortable bar and a good smell of broiled steak, and a cardroom with some intent poker players under the hooded green light.

We stood at the bar and he said, "A key for my friend, Clarence."

The bartender opened a drawer and took out a brass key and put it in front of me. "This is Mr. Travis McGee, Clarence. Trav, that key is good for life. Life memberships one dollar.

Give Clarence the dollar." I handed it over. "Cash on the line here for everything. No fees, no assessments, no committees. And a good steam room."

We picked up our drinks and I followed George over to a corner table. "We can eat right here when we're ready," he said. He frowned. "I just don't know what the hell to do about that girl."

"Didn't Gidge and Tommy work out fine?"

It startled him. "Yes. Sure."

"Don't worry about her. She's a very lush-looking kid, George. And probably as healthy as she looks. Probably if you knew everything about Gidge and Tommy at the same age, your hair would turn white."

"By God, if you were twenty years older, McGee, I'd hire you to watchdog her for what's left of the summer."

"You wouldn't be able to trust me."

"Anyway, whatever you came to see me about, consider it done. I owe you that much."

"I want information."

"It's yours."

"How much did Dave Berry steal overseas, how did he steal it and how did he smuggle it back into the States?"

It twisted him into another dimension so suddenly it was like yanking him inside out. His face turned a pasty yellow. His eyes darted back and forth as though looking for a place to hide. He opened his mouth three times to speak and closed it each time. Then he said, spacing the words, "Are you a Treasury Department investigator?"

"No."

"What are you?"

"I just try to get along, this way and that. You can understand that."

"I knew a Sergeant David Berry once."

"Is that the way you want it?"

"That's the way it has to be."

"What are you scared of, George?"

"Scared?"

"You can't be scared of Berry. He's been dead two years."

It startled him, but not enough. "Dead? I didn't know that. Did they let him loose before he died?"

"No."

"There's no secret of the fact I had to testify for him. I hadn't gotten out yet. I had to go to the presidio where they tried him. I said I'd served with him for two years and that he was a good competent noncom. I said I'd seen him lose his temper a lot of times, but he'd never hurt anybody before. He'd been drinking. A jackass lieutenant with brand-new gold bars, never been out of the States, didn't like the way Dave saluted him. He made Dave stand on a street corner and practice. After about five minutes of that, Dave just hit him. And then kept picking him up and hitting him again. And then he took off. If only he'd hit

him once, or if he hadn't run ... But I guess
you know all about it."

"Why should I? I want to know how much,
and how he got it and how he brought it back."

"I wouldn't know a thing about that, friend.
Not a single stinking thing."

"Because you made it the same way and
brought it back the same way, George?"

"I don't know what you're talking about,
believe me."

"Because you can't be sure there isn't
something official about this. Is that it?"

"McGee, I have had a lot of people asking a
lot of questions for a long time, and they all
get told the same thing. It was a good try,
McGee. Let's eat." His morale came back fast.

It was midnight when we left the back-street
club. He had a cocky, wary friendliness. As he
unlocked the door of the Lincoln and swung it
open, I chopped him under the ear with the
edge of my hand, caught him and tumbled him
in. And felt a gagging self-disgust. He was a
semi-ridiculous banty rooster of a man, vain,
cocky, running as hard as he could to stay in
the same place, but he had a dignity of existence which I had violated. A bird, a horse, a
dog, a man, a girl or a cat—you knock them
about and diminish yourself because all you do
is prove yourself equally vulnerable. All his
anxieties lay there locked in his sleeping skull,
his system adjusting itself to sudden shock,
keeping him alive. He had pulled at the

breast, done homework, dreamed of knight-hood, written poems to a girl. One day they would tumble him in and cash his in-surance. In the meanwhile it did all human dignity a disservice for him to be used as a puppet by a stranger.

He stirred once on the orderly trip back, and I found the right place on his neck for the thumb, and settled him back. Assured I was unobserved, I carried him into my chill nest, pulled the draperies, readied him for proof.

I stripped him, bound him, gagged him and settled him into the bottom of the shower stall. It was a hair piece. I peeled it away and tossed it onto the lavatory counter. It crouched there like a docile, glossy little animal.

A naked man who cannot move or talk, and does not know whether it is night or day, and is not told where he is or how he got there, will break very quickly.

The cold water brought him awake, and I let it run until I was certain he was thoroughly awake. I sat on a stool just outside the shower stall. I turned the water off. He was shivering. He stared at me with a total malevolence.

"George, do you think any government agency would permit this kind of interroga-tion? I've got several ways of getting rid of you completely. All perfectly safe. You've been asleep a long time, George. A lot of people are looking for you. But they're looking in all the wrong places. Kidnapping is illegal, George.

So we have to make a deal or I won't be able to let you go."

His eyes mirrored several new concerns, but he was telling himself he would never give in.

"I'm after Berry's little package, and I need your help. When you're ready to talk, just nod your head. Your only other choice is to get boiled like a knockwurst." I reached up and turned on the hot water. Good motels keep it at about a hundred and eighty degrees, and it doesn't take long to get there. I gave him a short burst and a cloud of steam. He bucked himself off the floor and screamed into the towel, a small noise. His eyes were maddened and bulging and he forgot to nod. I gave him a second blast, and when the steam cleared I could see him nodding vigorously. I gave him the third blast for insurance and he jumped nicely and nodded so hard he was rapping his head against the wall of the stall.

I reached in and took the gag away.

He groaned. "Jesus God, you've scalded me. What are you doing to me? My God, McGee, what are you trying to do?"

I reached my hand up and put it on the hot water lever.

"Don't!" he bawled.

"Keep your voice down, George. You're turning nice and pink. Now just talk to me. Tell me all about how you and Dave Berry worked it. And if something doesn't sound exactly right, I'll boil you a little, just for luck."

With a little coaching, he got through it pretty well. He and Berry had worked together from the beginning. At first it was Missionary Bonds, purchased in China, shipped back to a friend in the States to cash and send them the money to buy more. Double money on each deal. Then when that was closed out, it was the gold. They worked together, but kept the take separate. They didn't trust each other completely. But Berry was always making more than George Brell because he didn't spend an extra rupee on himself. He kept reinvesting it in gold. Berry found a goldsmith on Chowringhi Road in Calcutta who would cast facsimile structural parts of the aircraft out of pure gold. Berry would sand them a little, paint them with aluminum paint, screw them in place. A man in Kunming would melt them back into standard bars. This was after spot inspection was tightened up. When they were finally due to be shipped back on rotation, Brell had over sixty thousand American dollars, and he was certain that Dave Berry had at least three times that much. They took an R and R leave and hitched a flight down to Ceylon. It was Berry's idea. He had thought it all out, and had learned all he could about gem stones. The cash made Brell nervous. He followed Berry's lead. They spent the full ten days buying the most perfect gem stones they could find. Deep blue sapphires, star sapphires, dark Burmese rubies, star rubies. Some were too big to fit through the mouth of a standard-issue canteen. They cut the canteens open, put the gems inside and resoldered them. They poured melted wax over the stones to hold them in place. The wax hardened. They filled the canteens with water, hooked them on their belts and came home rich and nervous.

"I don't think they ever suspected Dave of a thing. He kept his mouth shut. But I did some hinting when I'd had a few drinks. They got onto me somehow. I went back home and hid them. I didn't dare touch them. I was on terminal leave, waiting to get out when I got called to the trial. After they sentenced him to life, I had a chance to be alone with him. I tried to make a deal with him. Tell me where his were. I'd take a reasonable cut for services rendered and see that his family got taken care of. Not a chance. He didn't trust me. He didn't trust anybody to be shrewd enough and smart enough. No, he was going to handle it himself without any hitches, and then he could make it all up to his wife and girls.

"I didn't touch mine for three years. Then I had to have cash. There was some land I had to pick up. I could buy it right. I couldn't run the risk of selling them in this country. Martha and I took a vacation. We went to Mexico. I made contacts there. I took a screwing, but at least I felt safe. I got just a little over forty thousand. I brought it back in U.S. dollars, and I fed it into the businesses a little bit at a time. I was careful. But they came down on me, on a net worth basis, trying to make a fraud charge stick, saying there was unreported income. And it has cost me a hundred thousand dollars to keep from being convicted for that lousy forty thousand. I couldn't talk to you. I couldn't take the chance. There's no statute of limitations on tax fraud, and they could still jail me for never declaring the money I made overseas. I'm marked lousy in the files, and they are after me every year. They're never going to stop. Now for God's sake, let me out of here."

After I untied him, I had to help him to his feet and half carry him into the bedroom. He sat on the edge of the bed and put his bald head down on his bare hairy knees and began to cry.

"I'm sick," he said. "I'm real sick, McGee."

He huddled and his teeth began to chatter. I tossed his clothes to him and he dressed quickly, his lips blue.

"Where are we?"

"About two miles from your house. We walked out of that club in Brownsville about three and a half hours ago. Nobody is looking for you."

He stared at me. "Do you know how you looked? You looked like you'd enjoy killing me."

"I didn't want to take too long over this, George."

"I couldn't hold out against what you were going to do."

"Nobody could, George."

He felt his bald head. "Where is it?"

"In the bathroom."

He tottered in. In a few moments he came out, hair piece in place. But the haggardness of his face made it look more spurious than before. He sat again on the edge of the bed. We were oppressor and oppressed. Traditionally this is supposed to create enmity. But, so often, it does not. It had opened up too many conflicting areas of emotions. The violence was a separate thing, like a wind that had blown through, and we were left with an experience shared. He was anxious to have me know that he had acquitted himself well. I was eager to have him believe he had left me no other choice.

"You are a friend of Callowell's?"

"No."

"I wrote the stuffy son of a bitch a nice letter and got a brush-off."

"I traced you through him."

He didn't seem to hear me. "Callowell was so damn nervous about anything cute. He'd check that airplane. He'd check around, and right over his fat head some of the static line braces would be solid gold. I tried to kid with Dave about it. Dave didn't see anything funny. He was dead serious about everything. God, it warted him to send money home when he knew he could keep it and keep on doubling it. I kept spending too much. I had a private car in a private garage in Calcutta. I had a wife

and two kids home too. But the difference between Dave and me, he was sure he'd live
forever." He shivered violently. "Trav, you
think you could get me home? I feel terrible."

I drove him home in the Lincoln. My rental
was in his drive, and the Triumph was there,
in the triple carport, beside a compact station
wagon. I rolled the Lincoln into the empty
space. Lights were on in the back of the house.
I went into the big kitchen with him. There
was a center island of stone, and copper pots
aligned on a fruitwood wall.

Gerry Brell came into the light wearing a
pink quilted robe with big white lapels, her
blonde hair tousled, eyes squinting in the
light.

"Honey, I don't feel so good," George said.

"He's having chills," I told her.

She took him off. At the doorway she turned
and said, "Wait for me, Trav."

I looked in the refrigerators and found Cold
Tuborg in the second one. I leaned against the
center island and drank it, feeling unreal. I
walked on a fabric of reality but it had an un-
comfortable give to it. You could sink in a
little way. If you walked too much and came to
a weak spot, you could fall through. I think it
would be pretty black down there.

After fifteen minutes she came back to the
kitchen, saw what I was having and got
herself one. She had brushed her hair and her
eyes were accustomed to the light.

She leaned against a bank of stainless steel sinks, facing me, and drank from the bottle and said, "He threw up. I turned on his electric blanket and gave him a sleeping pill."

"I think he's just emotionally upset."

"You've had a dandy introduction to the Brell family."

"Why did you ask me to stay?"

"Couldn't you just wait so we could work around to it instead of coming out with it like that?"

"I'm not at my best at four in the morning."

"Did you give him some bad news?"

"I don't know what you mean."

"George operates on the thin edge, and the edge is getting thinner all the time. I wanted to cut down the way we live, but he won't hear of it. Any little thing could tip the scales, and then the walls come tumbling down."

"How do you know that isn't exactly what I want?"

She looked rueful. "Then I made a bad guess about you. Did he say anything about me tonight?"

"No. But it's nice to know why you had me stay."

"What do you mean?"

"I hope you had a nice long talk with the girl when she got home."

"I guess I had to, didn't I? Not stepmother to child. That doesn't work, does it? Woman to woman. Call it an armed truce."

"The next time she makes a crack like that, Gerry, it might not go over his head."

"I think I made her understand that, if she loves her father, it would be a poor way to show it to give him a big broad hint about my infidelity. It's a hell of a confusing world, Mr. McGee. She's trying to throw herself away because she trusted me and I cheated on her father."

"Can she be sure of that?"

Her laugh was ugly. "Eyewitnesses are usually pretty positive. It happened back in June. Kids are so idealistic. How can I explain to her that it really didn't mean very much, that it was an old friend, sort of sentimental, unplanned, old-times-sake sort of thing. I don't make a habit of that sort of thing. But ever since I heard the door open and turned my head and saw her there, pale as death before she slammed the door and ran, I've felt cheap and sick about it. We were getting fond of each other up until then. Now she thinks I'm a monster. Tonight she was trying to hurt me by hurting herself. I just hope George has forgotten what she said. His judgment is bad enough lately without something like that to cloud it."

"He didn't make any mention of what she said."

"Good. Could this thing with Angie have made him so sick?"

"I think it's probable."

She tilted her pretty head and studied me. "Trav, you seem so mild and sure of yourself, and maybe you know enough about people to tell me what I should do about Angie."

"I'm not that sure of myself."

"I just wish there was a starting place. I can't reach her. She looks at me with hate. I just can't ever explain it to her."

"Are you a good human being, Gerry? I mean good in the sense that if you put everything in the scales, they'd tip that way?"

It startled her. "I don't know. I haven't thought of myself that way. I think I like the lush life a little too much. That's why I married George. I'm vain. I like men to admire me. I've got a coarse streak that comes out at the wrong times. But I do try to live up to . . . some kind of a better image of myself. And I try to improve. I came from nothing, Trav, from a little raggedy-ass spread in the Panhandle with too many kids and too few rooms. Dusted out, flooded out, burned out—we had it all. Until I got big enough to know that if I wore a tight skirt and red shoes, I could get the pretties I'd ached for, and then smart enough to know that the cheap approach gets the cheap pretties. This house and this life, they're big pretties, but the same old equation holds. I just don't know. Maybe I'm good, but that goddamn scale would hesitate a long time before tilting that way."

"Then tell the kid the whole thing. Lew proved she's old enough. Make her identify. Level with her. The saga of Gerry Brell, up to and including your little sentimental gesture,

and how you feel about her. Don't hold anything back. Don't let George send her away.
Keep her here until she knows it all and she
can balance it out herself."

"She'll despise me."

"She already does."

She brooded for a few moments. "I'll do no
sleeping tonight. I got to walk this one around,
boy." She set the empty bottle aside and said,
"I have the feeling I won't be seeing you
again."

"I have to see George once more."

nueve

MY motel windows were turning gray when I placed the overdue call to Chook. She was outraged, but when she calmed down she reported that Cathy lay listless on her hospital bed and answered questions in a small voice, in as few words as possible. And she liked Lois Atkinson. Very jumpy, sort of wild-eyed, but nice. They talked dance. Lois had studied ballet when she was little, but had grown too tall. And when was I coming back? That evening probably. Friday. The sun was visible from Florida, but it hadn't gotten to me. She was trying a replacement, temporary, for Cathy. The damned girl was fair, but she kept getting so winded you could hear her gasping forty feet away. Hurry home, darling McGee.

I slept until ten, arranged afternoon airline connections, then phoned my questions to a sly elderly angle-player in New York, an old friend, a quaint hustler of the unwary marks, a sometime dealer in everything from faked Braque to union dues, from gossip column items to guest shots. I said he would hear from me again.

I checked out and had a quick breakfast and went to George Brell's home. The pretty maid I had seen before had me wait inside the door while she checked with Mr. Brell. She came back and took me to him. He was propped up, reading the newspaper and drinking coffee. He was in a gigantic circular bed, with a pink canopy over it. In all the luxuriant femininity of that big bedroom, George looked shrunken and misplaced, like a dead worm in a birthday cake.

He threw the paper aside and said harshly, "Shut that door and pull that chair over here and sit down, McGee."

Pride quickly rebuilds the fallen walls. And refashions the past to fit its own requirements.

He stared at me. "You're very cute, boy. I'd done a lot of drinking, and I was upset about Angie, and I was exhausted from all the deals I've been making lately."

"I certainly took advantage of you, George."

"I did a hell of a lot of talking, and some of it I can't even remember. I've got some kind of a flu bug."

"And I was pretty rough, George."

"I want to know where we stand, McGee."

"In what way?"

"I'm warning you, boy, the worst mistake you can make is try to use anything against me. I'm not about to try to buy you off, if that's what you're after. I can get rough too. Damned rough."

"Are you planning on getting rough anyway?"

"I'm thinking about it."

"I guess if those tax people knew exactly where to look, and what historical facts they could check out, they could come back at you with a little more ammunition, George."

He swallowed and fumbled a cigarette out of his pack and said, "You're not scaring me. Not a bit."

"I think we ought to forgive and forget the whole thing, George."

He boggled at me. "You're not here to clip me?"

"Frankly I don't think you've got enough to be worth clipping, even if I went in for that line of work."

"I'm a rich man!" he said indignantly.

"George, you just live rich. Two years from now, if you've got a pot left, I'll be astonished. All I wanted from you was information, and I had to be sure you weren't being shifty. I'm after what Dave brought back. So far all that's been found was what was left of the canteen.

Not much, after eighteen years of tropical weather."

"Somebody got there first?"

"But they haven't had much of a start, George."

He tried a frail smile. "And that's all you wanted from me?"

"I tried to tell you that."

He sat up. "Any time you're in the Valley, Trav, this house is your house. You want to change your luck, I've got deals around here I just haven't had the time to work on. In ten years this area is going to be the most . . ."

"Sure, George."

He called to me as I reached the hall. I came back into the room. He moistened his lips. "If there should be any kind of trouble, and you have to do a lot of explaining . . ."

"I guess you better wish me luck."

He did and fell back into the percale pillows. As I started to find my way out, I looked back through the terrace glass toward the outdoor pool. Gerry and Angie were out there, standing on the far apron of the pool, talking intently, taking the sun before the day became too hot. Angie wore a conservative swim suit, and her stepmother wore a bikini. At that distance they looked of an age. After the promise of Gerry in clothing, her figure was a mild disappointment. She had high small breasts, and she was very long-waisted. The long limber torso widened into chunky hips and meaty thighs and short sturdy legs. As I watched them, Angie turned abruptly and started away. Gerry ran after her and caught her by the arm and stopped her. The girl stood in a sullen posture, her head lowered, as Gerry talked to her. Then she permitted herself to be led back to a sun cot. She stretched out, turning her face up toward the sun. The woman moved a white metal chair close and sat and talked down at the girl. Perhaps it was a trick of sunlight, but I thought I saw a silver gleam of moisture on the girl's cheek as I turned away.

This family was a circus act, balanced on a small platform atop a swaying pole, as the crowd goes *ahhhh,* anticipating disaster. A vain foolish man and a careless young wife and a tortured girl, swaying to the long drum roll. When it fell, the unmarked House Beautiful would sell readily, the Lincoln would be acquired by a Mexican dentist. Who would survive? George, perhaps, as he had the shortest distance to fall.

On the long east-southeast slant of the Houston-Miami jet flight, high over the blue steel silence of the Gulf, I thought of dour David Berry in the night, lifting away the big slabs of stone, tucking the shiny fortune down at the base of the pillar and replacing the stones, then waiting for his family to wake and find him. He had hoped for luck, stubbornly vowing to live and come back, knowing his women could not cope with the crafty problem of turning blue fire into money, knowing there was no one he could trust. Then Junior Allen had moved close to him, perhaps sensing a secret, chipping at it, prying.

Maybe, in his despair, David Berry had even considered trusting Junior Allen. But he had decided against it, or death came too quickly. But Allen knew it was there, and had lived there and thought and searched and finally found it.

A lump of wax like a huge blueberry muffin? All the rains and the heat and the salt damp had corroded the container away. And there would have been some bug with a taste for wax. Loose and gleaming probably, amid pale stalks and dirt, with Allen kneeling, his breath shallow and his heart thumping as he gathered them up.

Bugs would eat the wax. Chaw the old canvas. And one day there would be a mutation, and we will have new ones that can digest concrete, dissolve steel and suck up the acid puddles, fatten on magic plastics, lick their slow way through glass. Then the cities will tumble and man will be chased back into the sea from which he came. . . .

The large yellowed head lamps of Miss Agnes peered through dusk as I turned into Bahia Mar and found a slot a reasonable distance from the *Busted Flush*. There were lights on in my craft, a curiously homey look. Welcome traveler. I bing-bonged to save her unnecessary alarm, then stepped over the chain and went aboard, startling her when she pulled open the door to the lounge.

She backed away, smiling. "Hello. Or welcome home. Or something like that, Trav."

Three days had made an astonishing difference. Dark blue stretch pants patterned with ridiculous little yellow tulips. A soft yellow blouse with three-quarter sleeves. Hair shorter, face, arms and throat red-gold with new tan.

"Tourist!" I said.

"I thought maybe I wouldn't look so scrawny in this kind of . . ."

"Beach girl."

She drew herself up. "You think so? You think that's all there is to do?"

I had to be led around and I had to admire. Corridor walls scraped down and repainted a better color. New curtains in the head. A new set of stainless steel bowls for the galley. She said she would show me the topsides work by daylight when I could appreciate it.

I put my suitcase in my stateroom and came back into the lounge and told her she was a useful guest. We stood smiling at each other and then she leapt at me, clutched me, wailed once, and went away, snuffling, keeping her back toward me.

"What's wrong?"

"I don't know."

"Come on now, Lois. What's wrong?"

She pulled herself together quickly. "Does something have to be wrong? Maybe I'm glad to have you back. I don't know."

She had started to rebuild the woman things, the artifice, the indirection, the challenge. It was her pride at work. She was healing and I was glad to see it, and I did not want to nudge the structure too heavily. It was too new.

"I'll fix your drink," she said. "I sold the house."

"Got the money?"

"Soon."

"Sorry?"

"About the house? It's just a house. I was hiding down there in that wretched little village because I thought I'd been a bad wife." She brought me my drink and handed it to me.

"Aren't you getting a little fat, dear?" I asked.

She beamed. "A hundred and seven this afternoon."

"What's right for you?"

"Oh, one eighteen, one twenty." She patted her hip. "After one twenty it all goes here."

"So if the hiding is over, what are you going to do?" It was a fool question, tangle-footed and unimaginative. And no way to take it back. It made her aware of obligation. She could handle day by day. If she kept her head down. I had rocked the fragile new structure. Those dark and pleasantly tilted eyes became haunted and she sucked at her lips and knotted her hands. "Not right now," I said, trying to mend it. "Some day."

"I don't know."

"How was New York, Trav? New York was hot, Lois. How was Texas, Trav? Texas was hot, Lois. Did you have any fun, Trav? I wouldn't call it fun, Lois. I wouldn't know what to call it."

She measured me out one half of a smile. "Oh, shut up."

"Do I take you out tonight?"

"Oh, no! I cook, really."

I looked at my watch. "I have a hospital visit to make. So schedule it after I get back. Say forty minutes after I get back. Time to shower and change when I get back."

"Yes, master. Oh, I owe you six dollars and thirty cents on your phone bill."

"Those pants are pretty sexy, Mrs. Atkinson."

"I called Harp. I talked to Lucille. I didn't tell her hardly anything. Just that I'd been sick and things were better now."

"You're blushing, Mrs. Atkinson."

"Don't talk about these pants then. I bought them today. I don't feel very secure about them."

Cathy was in a six-bed ward. I pulled a chair close, kissed her on the forehead and sat beside her. I hoped she hadn't seen any dismay in my face. The sallow, thoughtful, rather pretty and fine-boned little face was gone. It was a stormy sunset, a ripe eggplant, a heavy mushroom. There was a single slit of brown eye to see with. Her left hand was splinted. "Hello," she said in a dead, fat-lipped voice. I stood up and yanked the curtains and sat down again and took her uninjured hand. It rested slack and warm and dry in mine.

"Junior Allen?" I said in a low voice.

"You don't have to mind about me, Mr. McGee."

"I thought it was Cathy and Trav.... Why did he do it?"

There is no way to read the expression of bruised meat. She watched me, hiding away back in there behind pain and indignity. "This part of it has got nothing to do with you."

"I want to know about it because you are my friend."

The slit eye was closed so long I began to wonder if she'd fallen asleep. She opened it. "He come there to the bar at the Bahama Room, and I messed up a routine awful when I saw him watching us. I don't know if it was an accident or he heard somehow or what. After, I hurried into my clothes and went out and he was gone. I went outside and saw him crossing the parking, and I ran after him. I caught him and said I wanted to talk with him. He said we didn't have anything to talk about. I said we could talk about money. That made him wonder. We walked through to the beach. Then I said that if he could just give me a little money out of what he got, maybe even just a thousand dollars, then I wouldn't make any trouble about any of the rest of it. He ask me what I would mean by trouble, and I said he found something that wasn't his, didn't he? He laughed once, short and nasty, and said I had no idea in the world what trouble was. So he reached quick and grappled holt of my neck with one hand, and pounded on my face with the other, and a couple of times he hit me in the belly. It all went dark while he was thumping on me, and I woke up in the ambulance. It . . . it doesn't hurt much now."

"Cathy, why didn't you tell the police?"

"I almost did."

"Why didn't you?"

"Not because I'm afraid of him beating on me again. But the whole thing might come out. And then I'd for sure never get a nickel back. And . . . it would have messed up what you're fixing to do, Trav. It could have messed you into a police thing."

What is there to do about one like that? I lifted her hand and kissed the roughened knuckles and said, "You are something, Cathy."

"I feel next door to nothing at all."

"Some good news anyway. There's no way to find out who the money ever belonged to, and no way to get it back to them anyway."

"What was hid there?"

"We'll talk when you get out of here."

"They won't tell me when. But I was on my feet some today. Hunched up and dizzy, but walked all the way to the john holding onto a lady. So maybe it won't be so long."

When I said goodby to her she said, "It was nice of you to come to visit me. Thank you very much."

I talked a long time with Lois that evening, giving her an edited version of my adventures. I went to bed. As I dropped off I could still hear her in the shower.

She came into my sleep and into my bed, awakening me with her mouth on mine, and strangely there was no shock or surprise in it. My subconscious had been aware that this would happen. A lady is a very special happening, so scented and delicate and breathless and totally immaculate. She wore a filmy something that tied at the throat and parted readily, presenting the warm length of her, the incredibly smooth texture of her, to my awakening embrace. Her breath was shuddering, and she gave a hundred quick small kisses. Her caresses were quick and light, and her body turned and glowed and glided and changed in her luxurious presentation of self, her mouth saying darling and her hair sweet in darkness, a creature in endless movement, using all of herself the way a friendly cat will bump and twine and nudge and purr. I wanted to take her on her basis, readying her as graciously as she had made herself ready, with an unhurried homage to all her parts and purposes, an intimate minuet involving offer and response, demand and delay, until the time when it would all be affirmed and taken and done with what, for want of a better name, must be called a flavor of importance.

But suddenly it was not going well. She would fall away from sweet frenzy, and then lift herself back up, but to a lesser peak. We were not yet joined. She was trying to hold onto all the wanting, but it kept receding, the waves of it growing smaller, her body becoming less responsive to each touch.

Finally she sobbed aloud and flung herself away, clenching her body into the foetal curl, posture of hiding, her back to me. I touched her. Her muscles were rigid.

"Lois, dear."

"Don't touch me!"

"Please, honey, you just . . ."

"Rotten, rotten, rotten!" she said in a small leathery howling voice, dragging the vowel sounds out.

I tried to stroke her. Her body was like wood, that great tension which comes with hysteria.

"Ugly rotten," she moaned. "You don't know the things, the ugly things. It can't ever be nice again. I let things happen. I did things. I stopped fighting."

"Give yourself time, Lois."

"*I . . . love . . . you!*" she wailed, protest and lament.

"You tried too soon."

"I wanted you."

"There's time."

"Not for me. I can't turn my mind off. It will always come back."

I laced my hands behind my head and thought about it. It was very touching. Such a total preparation. All plucked and perfumed, scrubbed and anointed, all tremulous with the reward for the heroic rescuer. Then, in the darkness, Junior Allen smirked at her and that sense of her own value, which a woman must have, was gone. She had packed and wrapped the gift with greatest care, labeled it with love, but suddenly it was a gift-wrapped flagon of slime. She had tried too soon, but had I tried to turn her away at the first touch, it might have been more traumatic than what had happened. I wondered if shock would be better than soothing.

"Terribly terribly dramatic, dear Lois."

"Uh?"

"So sad. Forever soiled, stained, lost, hopeless. The corrupted trollop of Candle Key. Gad, what drama!"

She uncurled herself slowly and cautiously, keeping her distance, furtively tucking the covering up under her chin. "Don't be a cruel disgusting bastard," she said in a flat voice. "At least try to have some empathy."

"For whom? A thirty-one-year-old adolescent, for God's sake? Do you think I'm so starved for a woman I take anything I can get? Sometimes I get a little foolish or a little

depressed, and I do just that, but it leaves a
bad taste. The bad taste comes from my being
an incurable romantic who thinks the
man-woman thing shouldn't be a contest on
the rabbit level. The rabbits have us beat. My
dear, if I thought you a bundle of corruptions,
what feast is that for a romantic? No, dear
Lois, you are sweet and clean from top to tippy
toe, fresh and wholesome in every part, and
pleasantly silly."

"Damn you!"

"I didn't tell you one little item, dear. It was
Junior Allen who beat up Cathy. In her words,
he grappled holt of her neck with one hand
and pounded on her face with the other. Until
she doesn't seem to have much of a face at the
present time. And she didn't turn him in, not
because she was scared, but because she
thought because I'm trying to help her I might
be brought into it somehow and the police
might mess me up somehow. I keep stacking
that up against your dramatics, and somehow
you don't come out too well. Try it yourself and
see."

She was silent for a long time. I could not
guess how she would respond, but I knew it
was a critical moment, perhaps the moment
upon which her whole future was balanced.
And I despised myself right along with all
other amateur psychiatrists, parlor sages,
barstool philosophers.

"But I've been sick!" she said in a teeny,
squeaky, ludicrous voice, and after a shocked
moment I recognized it as the tag line of that

ancient mouse joke, and I knew this girl would
be well. My laughter exploded, and in a moment she joined in. Like children, we laughed
ourselves into tears. It kept dying away and
beginning again, and I was glad to see she did
not water it down by trying to repeat it.

Then she got up, a pale and slender shape in
darkness, and found the diaphanous wrap and
floated it over her shoulders and was gone in
silence, but for the small click of my door
latch. Water ran. There was a thread of light
under my door. After a long time it went out. I
thought I knew by then how her mind would
work, and I waited. The door made the
smallest sound. The timid ghost drifted to me.
And it began as before.

Often she faltered, and I brought her back.
A lot of it was gentleness and waiting. And
being kind. And telling her of her sweetness.
At last there came the reward for patience, her
tremendous inhalation broken into six
separate fragments, her whole body listening
to itself then, finding, being certain, and then
taking with hunger.

Later she lay curled languid against my
chest, her heart and breathing slow. "Wasn't
too soon," she said, a blurred drone.

"No, it wasn't."

"Sweet," she said. "Ver' sweet." And she
nestled down into the sleep of total exhaustion.

I could have gone to sleep at once if I could
have convinced myself that everything was

just peachy fine. But I felt I had maneuvered myself into a rather nasty little corner. Where does responsibility stop? Do you buy the cripple a shoeshine box and send it out into the traffic? I had the feeling I now owned this sleeping thing. True, it was a splendid specimen, good bones, a true heart and a marvelous pelt. It could cook and adore and it had a talent for making love. Sew it into burlap and roll it in the mud and it would still be, unmistakably, a lady. You could take it anywhere.

But I wasn't built for owning, nor for anything which lasts. I could mend her spirit, only to go on and break her loving heart. And she would probably think it a poor bargain when the time came.

All the little gods of irony must whoop and weep and roll on the floors of Olympus when they tune in on the night thoughts of a truly fatuous male.

And I hold several international records.

diez

I did not know how she would be in the morning. I could only hope that she would not be bubbly, girlish and coy.

She was pouring juice when I went into the galley, and she turned gravely to be kissed, knowing it her due. A little tilt to the dark head. A flicker of appraisal in slanted eyes.

"Temperature normal, pulse normal, patient starving," she said.

"What?"

"McGee's clinic. Morning report. I'm having poached."

"Scrambled medium."

"Yessir."

The breakfast was rather silent, but not with strain.

After pouring second coffees, she sat and looked at me and said, "I'm being a hell of a problem to you, Trav."

"I worry about it every minute."

"Thank you for patience and endurance. You have won the Lois Award."

"Hang it with my other plaques."

"I watched the dawn from your sun deck. It was a nice one, with thunderheads. I came to the astonishing conclusion that I better not try to give anything until I've built up something to give. Otherwise, it's just taking."

"In the morning I'm often anti-semantic."

"Any future aggression, if there is any, will have to be yours."

"Sounds valid."

"And if there isn't any, don't go around worrying about what I might be thinking. Last night I collected on my assurance. In advance."

"Okay."

"Finish your coffee and come see what unskilled labor has done to your barge."

The work was worth the admiration I gave it. I shooed her off to the beach, with all her gear. She was back in three minutes just to tell me that she couldn't guarantee she wouldn't get a little nutty from time to time, but she felt she was past the pill period, and then she headed back toward the beach, a lissome broad in her mirrored sunglasses, walking on good legs, and she was far younger than her years, yet old as the sea she approached.

The operator tracked down Harry in New York, from one number to the next.

"In answer to your questions, laddy boy, it is mostly a yes. A few months back some very fine items made an appearance here and there, you might say classic items, the kind you expect there should be a description, like perhaps on an insurance list. But they are clean, I am told. All Asiatic items, with, as usual, some of the faceted stuff cut freehand enough to take a smidgen off the value. They have appeared here and there and worked their way up through the Street, everybody taking the small edge a quality thing brings, and they are by now mostly in the hands of the top houses being mounted in ways worthy of them, and you can find one advertised in *The New Yorker* as of present, page eighty-one, a retail to curl the three hairs I have remaining. It was a goodly number of top items, a minimum of ten, and perhaps no more than fifteen, unless somebody is holding tight. As to source, laddy boy, on the Street I found a word here, a word there, adding up to a smiling savage man, not by any means a fool, unloading one at a time, without haste, for cash, known to slam one man against a wall, and having no trouble thereafter, claiming he'd be back often with more of the same."

"What did he walk away with?"

"Forty thousand minimum. These are important items, laddy boy. And he would wait so proof could be had they were not hot. Cash sets up a certain discount situation, of course, but he played one against another, and did well."

"Could you do as well if you had the same kind of merchandise? Five per cent for your trouble?"

"You take my breath away. I might do even better. For ten."

"If I had them, we could dicker."

"You should not put such a strain on this ancient heart."

"Harry, can you get me a big blue star sapphire, say as big as the average he peddled, a fake that would slow an expert down for a few seconds?"

"There are only two kinds of fakes in that area, laddy boy, the very bad ones and the very good ones, and the good ones come high."

"How high?"

"Offhand, one large one."

"Can you rent one or borrow one and airmail it to me?"

"Switching is very unhealthy."

"It isn't what I have in mind."

"I might be able to arrange it."

"That isn't the question. I have faith in you. Can you arrange it today?"

"Dear boy!"

"I would hate to have to deal with anyone else, particularly if I get hold of anything genuine later on."

"My arm is twisted."

And then, with a thumb in the Yellow Pages, I began checking the marinas. All this great ever-increasing flood of bronze, brass, chrome, Fiberglas, lapstreak, teak, auto pilots, burgees, Power Squadron hats, nylon line, all this chugging winking blundering glitter of props, bilge pumps and self-importance needs dockside space. The optimum image is the teak cockpit loaded soft with brown dazed girls while the eagle-eyed skipper on his fly bridge chugs *Baby Dear* under a lift bridge to keep a hundred cars stalled waiting in the sun, their drivers staring malignantly at the slow passage of the lazy-day sex float and the jaunty brown muscles of the man at the helm. But the more frequent reality is a bust gasket, *Baby Dear* drifting in a horrid chop, girls sun-poisoned and whoopsing, hero skipper clenching the wrong size wrench in barked hands and raising a greasy scream to the salty demons who are flattening his purse and canceling his marine insurance.

But they have to park.

And while the outboarders have infinite choice, those that can house forty-footers are merely legion. I made over an hour of phone calls with the simple query, "Had the *Play Pen* in there lately, forty-foot Stadel custom?"

The assumptom was he'd put the damned thing somewhere handy when he'd visited the Mile O'Beach, but that assumption began to grow wan under the negative chorus. So somewhere unhandy, and I began to get into the toll call area, questing up and down the Waterway.

Lois came back from the beach. I sat glowering at the phone. She came back pinked, sun-dazed and slow moving, with spume-salted hair and a sandy butt, displaying upon a narrow palm, with a child's innocence, a small and perfect white shell, saying in a voice still drugged with sun and heat, "It's like the first perfect thing I ever saw, or the first shell. It's a little white suit of armor with the animal dead and gone. What does it mean when things look so clear and so meaningful? Silly little things."

I sat on a low stool, hating the phone.

"What's wrong?" she said, and leaned a hip against my shoulder, a weight oddly warm and heavy and luxurious for such slenderness. It was an uncontrived gesture and in a moment she was aware of it and moved away quickly, startled by herself.

"Where did Junior Allen like to tie up?"

She moved uneasily away, sat on a curve of the couch. "Little places, mostly. Not the great big marinas. I think he liked places where his boat would be biggest. A hose connection and power outlet and fuel. That's all he had to have. And privacy. He liked finger slips where he could tie up with the bow toward the main dock."

"I've been trying the small ones too."

"But after what he did to Mrs. Kerr, wouldn't he go away?"

"I would think so. But where was he beforehand? He couldn't have known that was going to happen. I'd assume he'd move along, thinking she would tell the police."

"Back to the Bahamas?"

"Maybe. I thought I could find where he was, and ask around and get some idea where he was headed. Did he ever say anything about things he wanted to do, or places he wanted to go?"

"He said something one time about going around the Gulf Coast and over to Texas."

"Oh fine."

"Trav, you know he could be tied up at some private place, like he was tied up at my dock."

"That's a lot of help too."

"You asked me. I'm trying to help."

She looked at me with gentle indignation. She was what we have after sixty million years of the Cenozoic. There were a lot of random starts and dead ends. Those big plated pea-brain lizards didn't make it. Sharks, scorpions and cockroaches, as living fossils, are lasting pretty well. Savagery, venom and guile are good survival quotients. This forked female mammal didn't seem to have enough tools. One night in the swamps would kill her. Yet behind all that fragility was a marvelous toughness. A Junior Allen was less evolved. He was a skull-cracker, two steps away from the cave. They were at the two ends of our bell curve, with all the rest of us lumped in the middle. If the trend is still supposed to be up, she was of the kind we should breed, accepting sensitivity as a strength rather than a weakness. But there is too much Junior Allen seed around.

"Find me that boat," I told her.

"What do you mean?"

"What specific or general thing do I have to know that will enable me to locate it?"

She stood up slowly and thoughtfully and went off to take her shower. I knew it was an emotional strain for her. She was trying to wipe every memory of that period out of her mind. And now I was forcing her to remember. They would be tangled memories, filtered through alcohol.

Suddenly she came racing into the lounge. She wore one of my big blue towels in sarong fashion, and had a white towel wrapped around her head. Her face looked narrow and intent. Her features looked more pointed.

"That last trip," she said. "I don't know if it will help. We stopped at some sort of a boat yard in Miami. I can't even remember the name. Something about a new generator. He kept complaining about the noise the generator made. They took up the hatches and got down in the bilge and did a lot of measuring. The man said it would take a long time to get the one Junior Allen wanted. It made him

angry. But he ordered it anyway. He left a
down payment on it. He ordered some kind of
new model that had just been introduced."

She sat beside me and we looked at the
Yellow Pages. She ran a slender fingertip
down the listings. She stopped. "That's it.
That's the one."

Robinson-Rand, down below Dinner Key, off
the Ingraham Highway. Shipyard, storage. No
job too large, no job too small.

"Maybe it hasn't come in yet," she said in a
thin little voice. She shivered. "I'm scared,
Trav. I hope it came in and he got it and went
away. I hope you never find him."

I had bought Lois a lunch and sent her back
to the houseboat. I parked Miss Agnes in
Robinson-Rand's sizable lot. Even in the summer doldrums, it was a brisk place. Their
storage areas looked full. They had long rows
of covered slips, and two big in and out structures for small craft. The shop areas were in
big steel buildings. Saws and welding torches
and power tools were in operation, even on a
Saturday afternoon, but I could guess it was
only a skeleton crew working. They had a lot
of big cradles and hoists, slips and ways. The
office area was built against one end of one of
the shop buildings, near a truck dock.

There was one girl working in the office, a
plump, impersonal redhead with one eye
aimed slightly off center.

"We're not really open," she said.

"I just wanted to check on a generator that was ordered, find out if it has come in yet."

She sighed as though I had asked her to hike to Duluth. "Who placed the order?" Sigh.

"A. A. Allen."

She got up and went over to a bank of file cabinets. She began rifling through cards. "For the *Play Pen?*" Sigh.

"That's right."

She took the card out and frowned at it. "Ordered June second. That's a Kohler 6.5A-23. Goodness, it should be in by now."

"Doesn't it say on the card?"

"No, it doesn't say on the card." Sigh. "All I can tell from the card is that it hasn't been delivered or installed." Sigh.

"Does the card say who handled the order?"

"Of course the card says who handled the order." Sigh. "Mr. Wicker. He isn't here to-day."

"Joe Wicker?"

"No. Howard Wicker. But people call him Hack."

"Do you keep a running list of the boats you have in?"

"Of course we keep a running list of the boats we have in." Sigh. "Down at the dock office."

"Of course you keep a running list of the boats you have in. Down at the dock office. Thanks a lot."

She looked momentarily disconcerted. "Excuse me. The air conditioning isn't working right. And the phone keeps ringing. And people keep coming here." Sigh.

"I'm sorry too. Be of good cheer, Red."

She smiled and winked the crooked eye and went back to her gunfire typing.

I phoned the only listing for a Howard Wicker from a chilly saloon. A very small child answered and said, "Hello." No matter what I said, it kept saying hello. I kept asking it to get its daddy and it kept saying hello, and I began to feel like Shelley Berman. Then the child gave a sudden howl of anguish and a woman with a tense exasperated voice came on the line.

Hack was out in the yard. Hold the line. The child came back on and started giving me the hello again. Tearfully.

"Yes?" Wicker said.

"Sorry to bother you on your day off. I understand you installed a Kohler 6.5A-23 on a forty-foot Stadel custom, and I'd like to know how it worked out."

"What? Oh. I don't know what you mean. It's a good rig. If there's room for it, and you don't hit over a seven thousand watt peak demand, it's going to be okay, isn't it?"

"I mean noise and vibration and so on."

"It's quiet enough for that rating. You're asking about a boat called the *Play Pen*?"

"I think that's the name."

"We got the generator in last Monday or Tuesday, and it hasn't been installed yet. They've phoned in a few times asking about it. I expect they'll phone in again this week. Then bring the boat around and we'll put it in. You want to see how the job goes, I could let you know. What have you got now?"

"An old Samson 10KW diesel. Manual and noisy. And big."

"It would depend on peak load, if you could get along with less."

I told him I would appreciate it if he'd give me a ring when the appointment with the *Play Pen* was set up. A collect call in Lauderdale. He wrote the number down and said he would.

"It won't be too long, will it?" I asked. "The *Play Pen* is in the area?"

"Far as I know. He knows it's due about now."

I drove back through late afternoon heat. The world darkened, turned to a poisonous green, and somebody pulled the chain. Water roared down the chute. Rose-colored lightning webbed down. Water bounced knee high, silver in the green premature dusk, and I found a place to pull off out of the way and let the fools gnash each other's chrome and tin-work, fattening the body shops, busying the adjustors, clogging the circuit court calendars. The sign of the times is the imaginary whiplash injury.

Miss Agnes squatted, docile under the roar of rain, and I tried to pull Junior Allen into fo-

cus. Like the most untidy little hoodlum
knocking over a Friendly Bob Adams Loan Office, he was on a short rein. Or reign. In these
documented times, where we walk lopsided
from the weight of identifications, only the
most clever and controlled man can hope to exist long on a hijacked fortune. And Junior
Allen was a felon. Maybe he was clever, but
certainly not controlled. Returning to Candle
Key to rape and corrupt the lonely woman who
found him distasteful had been foolish.
Bashing Cathy had been idiotic. Showing gems
to the little Haitian bitch had been the act of a
careless, overconfident man. He was a
swaggering sailor with money in his pocket,
and if he kept on being careless, neither he nor
the money could last very long. Viewed in that
light, his luck was impressive. His victims,
thus far, had kept their mouths shut. Perhaps
his present victim, whoever she might be,
might not be so obliging. And I might not have
very much time.

A sulphur sun pierced the gloom, and the
rain stopped and I drove to the hospital. She
could look at me out of both eyes now, and the
shape of her mouth looked more familiar.
Chook had brought her a pretty new robe.
With the nurse's permission, she moved from
the bed into a wheel chair, and I pushed her to
the sun room at the end of the corridor.

"Tomorrow I can go home," she said.

I moved a chair closer to her. Old bruises
turn green and yellow. The old swelling kept

her brown eyes pinched small. "Maybe I'm going to catch up with him soon, Cathy."

"What are you going to do?"

"Play it by ear."

"I'd like it fine if you could kill him some way you wouldn't get into trouble about it."

"I didn't know you were so savage about it."

"Savage? I'm not savage about it at all. The way that man does you, he's better dead. I was plain foolish, Trav. Even after everything, I was still hoping. You know? He'd find out it was best he should be back with me. Now wasn't that dumb? I couldn't even let myself know that was what I was wishing on. Then when he taken me and hammering me there in the dark, nobody to hear, not caring if he killed me dead, that killed it for good. I saw his face once when he'd spun me toward the palm tree lights, and he was smiling."

"Had he come looking for you?"

"He didn't say."

"Do you think he did?"

"I think it was just accident. There aren't so many places with a summer show, and a man roving around could come there and be as surprised as I was to see him. Trav, you be careful getting near him. He's mean as anything you like to find in a swamp."

"I'll be careful."

"I have the feeling he's not long for this world, and I don't want him taking you with him when he goes. I think when they had him locked away for five years, something went wrong with him. Something stopped. Something other people have. And he's sly. He must have tricked my daddy, and my daddy was real sly hisself, they say." She stared thoughtfully at me. "I guess you have to be a sly man too. Your face doesn't show much. But go careful with him, like as if he's a snake."

I got back to the *Busted Flush* at six-thirty. The rain had washed the sunset time to a lambent beauty. A fine east wind had driven the bug life inland. Scores of little groups were cocktailing aboard their craft, lazy-talking, working themselves into Saturday night. Buddy Dow, hired skipper of a big lunker owned by an insurance company in Atlanta, had enlisted two recruits and was despairingly in need of more. He tried to enlist me, and I paused for a moment to say no politely. He had them primed. A plain hello was a comedy line that set them all giggling. What Buddy calls the dog-ratio ran pleasantly low on this group. I had the feeling that if I got too close, greedy secretarial hands would haul me aboard, kicking and screaming. They all work toward a memorable vacation.

I went on along to my broad scow, and for a time it seemed as if she wasn't going to unlock it and let me inside. When she did, she went running to the couch and threw herself face down, rigid.

"What's the matter with you?"

An agony had blanched and dwindled her face. "He's here," she whispered.

"Junior Allen?"

"He saw me."

She was too upset to be very coherent, but I got it all out of her. She had gone down to the marine supply place to look for some kind of a small present for me. Just to give me a present. And she had wandered out onto the gas dock just beyond the offices and the tall control tower for the marina. And the *Play Pen* had been there, gassing up. Junior Allen had straightened up, stared at her, grinned at her, and she had fled.

"He didn't follow you?"

"No. I don't think so."

"Was he alone?"

"No."

"Who was with him?"

"I don't know. Young people. Three or four. I don't know. All I could see was him."

"What time was all this?"

"A-about quarter after five, I think."

once

WILLY Lazeer is an acquaintance. His teeth and his feet hurt. He hates the climate, the Power Squadron, the government and his wife.The vast load of hate has left him numbed rather than bitter. In appearance, it is as though somebody bleached Sinatra, skinned him, and made Willy wear him.

I knew he was off at six, and I knew it took him an hour of beer to insulate him against going home, and I knew where he would be loading up. I sat beside him at the bar. He gave me a mild, dim glance of recognition. His hour was almost up. I prodded his memory.

"*Play Pen. Play Pen.* Sure, I seen that to-day."

175

"Forty-foot Stadel custom, white topsides, gray hull, blue line. Skippered by a rugged brown guy with white curly hair and small blue eyes and a big smile."

"So?"

"I was wondering where he's docked."

"How should I know, McGee? How the hell should I know?"

"But you do remember him?"

"He paid cash."

"Stopped a little after five?"

"So?"

"What kind of people did he have aboard, Willy?"

"Smart-ass kids."

"Tourists, college kids?"

He stared through me for a moment. "I knew one of them."

"One of the kids?"

"What the hell are we talking about? One of the kids. Yes. You know over the bridge on the right there, past where they're building is a place called Charlie Char-Broil."

"I know the place."

"I seen her there as a waitress. Young kid. They got their names on little badges. Hers is a funny one. Deeleen. I ain't seen her there a couple months. How come I remember her, she got snotty with me one time, bringing me the wrong order."

It was as far as he could go with it.

I went back to Lois. She had a glass of bourbon that looked like a glass of iced coffee. Her smile was loose and wet and her eyes didn't track. I took it away from her and took her into her stateroom. She made little tired singing sounds and lurched heavily against me. I tipped her onto the bed and took her shoes off. In three minutes she was snoring.

I locked up and went off on a Deeleen hunt.

Charlie Char-Broil smelled of burned grease, and she didn't work there any more. But a friend named Marianne did, a pretty girl except for a rabbit mouth she couldn't quite manage to close. Nineteen, I guessed. Once she was convinced I wasn't a cop, she joined me in a back booth.

"Dee, she got fired from here when they changed the manager. The way it was, she did anything she damn pleased, you know? The manager we had, he was all the time taking her back in the storeroom, and finely somebody told the company. I told her it was the wrong way to act. She had a couple other jobs and they didn't last and I don't see her much any more. I did see her. But, I don't know, some things can get too rough, you know what I mean? Fun is fun, but it gets too rough. What I found out, on a blind date she got for me, geez, it was a guy like could be my father, you know? And there was a hell of a fight and I found out she took money from him for me to show up. I ask her what she thinks I am anyhow. I think she's going to get in bad trouble, and I don't want to be around, you know."

"Where does she live?"

"Unless she's moved—she moves a lot—she's in the Citrus Inn. It's up like opposite Deerfield Beach, kind of an apartment-hotel kind of thing, sort of old and cruddy. In 2A up there, with a girl named Corry, that's where she was last I knew, getting her unemployment."

That was all the time she could spend with me. She slid out of the booth, patting at the blue and white skirt of her nylon uniform. She seemed to hear the total effect of her own words, and looked a little disconcerted. She was a strong-bodied girl whose rather long neck and small head made her look more delicately constructed than she was. Her fine silky hair was a soft brown with bleached streaks. "Don't get me wrong about Deeleen," she said. "I don't want you should think I'm trine to cut her up. The thing is, she had an unhappy love affair when she was just a kid."

"How old is she now?"

"Oh, she's twenty now." She hesitated. She was obligated to end our little chat with a stylized flourish. The way it's done in serial television. So she wet her little bunny mouth, sleepied her eyes, widened her nostrils, patted her hair, arched her back, stood canted and hip-shot, huskied her voice and said, "See you aroun', huh?"

"Sure, Marianne. Sure."

Bless them all, the forlorn little rabbits. They are the displaced persons of our emotional culture. They are ravenous for romance, yet settle for what they call making out. Their futile, acne-pitted men drift out of high school into a world so surfeited with unskilled labor there is competition for bag-boy jobs in the supermarkets. They yearn for security, but all they can have is what they make for themselves, chittering little flocks of them in the restaurants and stores, talking of style and adornment, dreaming of the terribly sincere stranger who will come along and lift them out of the gypsy life of the two-bit tip and the unemployment, cut a tall cake with them, swell them up with sassy babies, and guide them masterfully into the shoal water of the electrified house where everybody brushes after every meal. But most of the wistful rabbits marry their unskilled men, and keep right on working. And discover the end of the dream. They have been taught that if you are sunny, cheery, sincere, group-adjusted, popular, the world is yours, including barbecue pits, charge plates, diaper service, percale sheets, friends for dinner, washer-dryer combinations, color slides of the kiddies on the home projector, and eternal whimsical romance—with crinkly smiles and Rock Hudson dialogue. So they all come smiling and confident and unskilled into a technician's world, and in a few years they learn that it is all going to be grinding and brutal and hateful and precarious. These are the slums of the heart. Bless the bunnies. These are the new people, and we are making no place for them. We hold the dream in front of them like a carrot, and finally say sorry you can't have any. And the schools where we teach them non-survival are gloriously architectured. They will never live in places so fine, unless they contract something incurable.

I went north of the mainland route, past an endless wink and sputter of neon, through the perpetual leaf-fall and forest floor of asphalt, cellophane, candy wrappers, Kleenex, filter tips, ticket halves, Pliofilm and latex. One of Junior Allen's women lay wounded and the other lay drunk, and I was looking for a third.

The Citrus Inn was an old place, a three-story cube of cracked and patched Moorish masonry, vintage 1925, with three entrances, three sets of staircases, three stacks of small apartments. It was on a short, dead-end street in a commercial area. It was across the street from a large truck depot, and bracketed on one side by a shoestring marina and on the other by a BEER-BAIT-BOATS operation which had a tavern specializing in fried fish sandwiches. There was a narrow canal behind the three structures, sea-walled, stagnant.

The Citrus Inn had its own eroding dock, parallel to the sea wall. I had parked in front. I walked around the unlighted side of the Citrus Inn. I stopped abruptly and moved off into deeper shadows. There were two darkened old hulks tied up to the Citrus Inn dock. The third craft was lighted inside, and a weak dock light shone against the starboard side of it and into

the cockpit. It shone on the life ring. The *Play
Pen*. There were several of them in the cockpit.
I couldn't see them distinctly. They had music
going, the hesitating rhythms of Bossa Nova.
A girl moved to it. Another girl laughed in a
slurred sour way. A man said, in a penetrating
voice, "Dads, we are just about now out of beer
and that is a hell of a note, Dads. Somebody
has got to trek way the hell to Barney's. You
going to do us like this in the islands, Dads?
You going to let us run out of the necessities of
life once we get over there?"

Another man rumbled some kind of an
answer, and a girl said something which the
music obscured. In a few moments two of them
came by me, heading for the tavern. I saw
them distinctly when they clambered up onto
the dock, a husky, sideburned boy with a dull
fleshy face, and a leggy awkward girl in
glasses.

As they passed me the girl said, "Shouldn't
you buy it one time anyway, Pete?"

"Shut up, Patty. It makes Dads happy to
spring for it. Why spoil his fun?"

I had my first look at Junior Allen. It wasn't
much of a look. He was a shadowy bulk in the
cockpit of the boat, a disembodied rumble of a
voice. A single bark of laughter.

When I got back to the *Busted Flush*, Lois
was still out. I sat her up. She whined at me,
her head heavy, her eyes closed. I got her up
and took her over to the beach and walked her

until she had no breath for complaining. She trudged along, dutiful as a naughty child. I walked her without mercy, back and forth, until her head was clear, and then we sat on a public bench to give her time to catch her breath.

"I've got a ghastly headache," she said in a humble voice.

"You earned it."

"I'm sorry, Trav. Really. Seeing him ... scared me so."

"Or gave you an excuse?"

"Don't be hateful."

"I just don't like to see you spoil what you're trying to do."

"It won't happen again."

"Do you mean that?"

"I don't know. I don't *want* it to happen again. But I keep thinking ... he could come walking along this beach right now."

"Not tonight. He's busy."

"What!"

I told her how and where I had found him. With a sideburned boy named Pete, and three girls named Deeleen, Patty and Corry.

"From the little I heard, he's taking all of them or some of them on a cruise to the Bahamas. They think they're working him. They think they've found a very soft touch. They call him Dads."

"Can't those poor kids see what he is?"

"Cathy didn't. You didn't."

"What are you going to do?"

"Go see if I can make a date tomorrow afternoon."

"They might be gone."

"I think he'll wait until he gets the new generator installed."

"But what if he leaves with them in the morning?"

"If that seems too dreadful to you, Lois, you can always get drunk."

"You don't have to be so cruel."

"You disappointed me."

"I know. I'm sorry."

"How's your head now?"

"A little better, I think. Trav?"

"Yes, honey."

"Trav, I'm so hungry I could eat this bench."

When I took a look at the outdoors Sunday morning I knew they weren't going anywhere. It was a sparkling day. The wind had swung around and it was coming out of the northeast, hard and steady. A wind like that builds too much of a chop out in the Stream for anything the size of Junior Allen's cruiser. It would be running seven or eight feet out there, and very dirty.

I waited until noon and then drove up to the Citrus Inn. Apartment 2A was in the center section on the second floor. I wore a courting costume, summer version. T shirt, khaki slacks, baseball cap, straw shoes, an eager smile, and a bottle of good bourbon in a brown paper bag. I rapped on the scarred and ornate old wooden door, and rapped again, and a girl-voice yelled in an exasperated tone, "Just a minute!"

The latch rattled. The door opened an inch and a half, and I saw a tousle of dark hair and a segment of tan face and a cold green unfriendly eye. "Whaddya want?"

"I'm looking for Deeleen."

"She's not here."

"Are you Corry?"

"Who the hell are you?"

"A friend of a friend."

"Like who?"

"Marianne, works at Charlie Char-Broil."

"That silly bitch hasn't got any friends."

Had I done any pleading or begging, she would have slammed the door. So I stood easy, mildly smiling. It's a relaxed area. There is a code for all the transients. If you are presentable, unhurried, vaguely indifferent, it is a challenge. I was having better luck with this than I expected, up to this point. I wanted it to continue. If you push against hostility and suspicion, you merely increase it. In a few moments I saw a little less animosity.

"What's with this Marianne and you looking for Deeleen? I don't get it."

"I don't want to confuse you, Corry."

"There's some facts of life I should know?"

"I used to see Deeleen around there and never got to know her, and then she left and I was wondering about her, if she'd left town, and I asked around and Marianne said maybe she was still here. So this was an empty day, and I had this jug, so I thought I would come see. But if she's as friendly as you are, I guess it wasn't much of an idea."

She examined me for at least twenty silent seconds. "Stick around a minute," she said, and closed the door. It was ten minutes before she came out. She had stiffened her dark hair somehow until it looked like a Japanese wig. She wore a swim suit and an open cabana coat. The swim suit was a black and white sheath, the black faded and the white slightly grubby. Though flawed by a bulldog jaw and a little too much meat across the hips, she was reasonably presentable. She closed the door and smiled up at me and said, "You're practically a giant, huh? You got a name?"

"Trav."

"There's a kid in the apartment sleeping it off. She was whoopsing half the night from beer. Come on, I'll show you something."

I followed her down the short corridor to a back window overlooking the dock. A girl in a very brief bikini lay on a pad on the cabin roof of the *Play Pen*. I looked down at her over Corry's shoulder.

She looked up at me quizzically. "I don't blame you at all to come looking, she's built so cute, huh?"

"Tasty."

"But if she's absolutely the only idea you

came up here with, honey, you can save yourself the trouble. She's all set up with the guy owns the boat."

"It's a lot of boat. Whose is it?"

"An old guy named Allen. We call him Dads. We're going to go far and wide on that boat, man. We're going to the Bahamas on that boat. Would you believe it, he says it's hard to find people to go cruising with you? Isn't that a crazy problem. But the way things are, honey, she won't play. It could screw up the boat ride." She turned toward me from the window with just the slightest hint of the stylized posture of the model, the small mechanics of display, seeking approval. "So?"

She had invited inspection and I gave it, then said, "You have to know when to change your ideas. You have to stay loose."

"The thing is," she said, "I wouldn't want you should have any terrible disappointment. I mean on account of Dee."

This was the small smoky game of appraisal and acceptance, offer and counter-offer. She had narrowed it down to that one response necessary to her esteem. So I responded as she wished. "If that was you down there in the sun, Corry, and Dee up here with me, then I could feel disappointed."

She smirked and beamed and preened, then linked my arm and took me down onto the dock. "Hey!" she said. Deeleen sat up, owlish in huge black glasses. "Where is everybody?" Corry asked as I helped her aboard.

"Dad took off someplace in Pete's car. Pete went down to see Mitch about if he's got the motor back on the little boat yet. Patty okay?"

"She's still sacked out up there."

Deeleen got up and came clambering slowly and cautiously down into the cockpit. At a thirty-foot distance she was a very attractive, ripe-bodied young girl. At close range the coarseness, and the sleaziness of the materials used in construction were all too evident. Her tanned hide had a coarse and grainy look. Her crinkle of putty-colored hair looked lifeless as a Dynel wig. The strictures of the bottom half of the bikini cut into the belly-softness of too many beers and shakes, hamburger rolls and french fries. The meat of her thighs had a sedentary looseness. Her throat and her ankles and the underside of her wrists were faintly shadowed with grime. There was a coppery stubble in her armpits, and a bristle of unshaven hair on her legs, cracked red enamel on her toenails. The breast band of the bikini was just enough askew to reveal a brown new-moon segment of the nipple of her right breast.

"Deeleen, I want you should meet Trav," Corry said.

"Hi," Deeleen said, looking me over. She had a broad mouth and a pink stain of lipstick on one front tooth. She was obviously awaiting further identification.

"That Marianne works at the Char-Broil, she told him one time we were out this way, and he came around. I was telling him about going on the cruise with Dads." It was very casual, but totally explicit. He came looking for you, but I told him the score and he settled for me.

Deeleen gave a little shrug of acceptance and slumped into a canvas chair, spraddled and hot. There was a little roll of fat around her waist. She hitched the bikini top up. High against the meat of the insides of her thighs a fringe of pubic hair escaped the scanty fabric which encased the plump and obvious pudendum. A few years ago she would have been breathtakingly ripe, and even now, in night light, with drinks and laughter, there would be all the illusions of freshness and youth and desirability. But in this cruelty of sunlight, in this, her twentieth year, she was a record of everything she had let them do to her. Too many trips to too many storerooms had worn the bloom away. The freshness had been romped out, in sweat and excess. The body reflects the casual abrasions of the spirit, so that now she could slump in her meaty indifference, as immunized to tenderness as a whore at a clinic.

"What's with squirrel-face Marianne?" she asked indifferently.

"Nothing new."

Corry shed her cabana coat, put canvas cushions on the wide transom and stretched out. They had stopped surveying me. I had passed inspection.

"Even with that wind it's almost too goddamn hot," Corry said. "Anybody figured out what we're going to do?"

"I'll wait'n see what Dads wants."

Corry turned more toward Dee, closing me out of the conversation. "Was it the way you figured?" she asked.

Dee gave a flat, mirthless laugh. "Only more so."

"Anybody want a drink?"

They both stared at me as though startled to find I was still there. "Sure," Deeleen said. "What is it?"

"Bourbon."

"Okay," Corry said.

"But he locked it when he took off," Dee said. "You can't get down where the ice and glasses and stuff is. Corry, you want to bring stuff down from upstairs?"

"It's after one," Corry said. "He can get some stuff from Barney, can't he?"

"Ask to buy some of the big paper cups," Dee told me. "And get a six-pack of Coke, huh?"

Barney's service was slow, and he overcharged me for the cups, Coke and ice. By the time I returned to the *Play Pen,* the girls had shuffled me and dealt me. Corry informed me of their approval and of the choice that had been made. She did it by rubbing the back of my neck while I fixed her drink. We moved back under the overhang, out of the direct weight of the sun. With the breeze, it was comfortable. As they began to get a little high, they included me more naturally in their conversation. We walked about the cruise. Pete arrived. He had a dead handshake, like a canvas glove full of hot sand. Corry gave him a key to 2A and he went up to see how Patty was. There was discussion about whether she would go on the cruise. She would have to lie to her folks.

Suddenly Junior Allen swung aboard, leaped, landed lightly. He was immaculate in white sport shirt, white slacks, pale blue yachting cap. I guessed he was nearing forty. I had not been prepared for him to look so powerful and so fit. He was broad, with shoulders so packed and corded with muscle they gave him a slightly simian posture, the impression enhanced by the extra-long weight and heft of brown tattooed arms, and the short legs, slightly bowed. He had a brown, seamed, knotty face, broad, smiling broadly, the smile squinching the small blue eyes. It was a friendly grin. It was a likable grin. It did not change in any way as he looked at me.

"Hello, kids," he said. His voice was a brassy rumble. He rumpled Dee's lifeless hair with a big brown paw. "Who we got aboard, little sweetheart?"

She was transformed. She was elfin, lisping, adoring, his ripe, dumpy little child. "This is Trav, darling. He's with Corry. Trav, this is Dads Allen. He's the one owns this boat. Hasn't it got a cute name?"

"It's a *very* cute name," I said.

He was quick. He caught my hand in exactly the way I didn't want him to catch it, and watched my mouth as he ground my knuckle bones.

"Glad you like it," he said. "Welcome aboard."

He took his keys out and unlocked the hatchway to the cabins. He pulled Dee to her feet, slapped her bare rump and said, "Little sweetheart, you go bring up some decent glasses and the vodka."

Little sweetheart snickered and arched and went below dutifully. Junior Allen sat where she had been, and patted Corry's bare knee and said, "What's your line of work, Trav?"

"Whatever I happen to find. A little charter boat work in season. Take boats north and south for the winter folks. Fry cook. Half-ass marine mechanic. You name it."

After little sweetheart brought his bottle and the glasses, he fixed himself a drink. He beamed at me. "These kids tell you about the trip? I'm going to take four of 'em over and show them the islands. Hell, I've got the boat, the time and the money. It's the least I can do."

Had I not known the history, I would have readily bought the image he was projecting. Fatuous, expansive idiot, hooked by the tired flesh of little sweetheart, taking her and three of her friends on the romantic tropic tour.

"Passenger list still open?" I asked, smiling back.

That changed his eyes but not his grin. "If Pete and I sleep in the two bunks forward, that leaves the main cabin for the gals. I can sleep six, but they got to be very good close friends." He roared with laughter. "Sorry we can't sign you on, buddy."

"I get to be the fifth wheel," Corry said bitterly.

"How so, girl?"

She stared coldly at him. "What's so complicated, Dads. You and Dee, Pete and Patty. And good old Corry. Hell, sign him on. I'll need somebody to talk to. Maybe you'll need somebody to run your boat."

"I never need any help with a boat," he said, smiling. "Or anything else, little sweetheart."

"I'm Corry. She's little sweetheart, Dads."

He patted her knee again and beamed at her. "You'll have fun. Don't you worry about it a minute."

"Always bitching about something," Dee said. "Always."

Pete and Patty came aboard. And within minutes I knew what Junior Allen was after. At first glance Patty was unattractive, an impression derived from the gawkiness and the glasses. They kidded her coarsely about getting sick, and she responded by clowning. The clowning was her defense. Her breasts were high and immature and sharp against the fabric of her blouse. Her legs were long and pale and lovely. There was a colt grace about

the book and long after the shower had
stopped, I heard her calling me in a small
voice. I went to the bedroom. She had pulled
the yellow shades down, making a dim golden
light in the shabby room. She lay naked on the
bed with a black towel across her loins. "Hello
there, darling," she said. She wore the same
smile as in the photographs, but drowsier.

"Hello yourself."

Wrestler's jaw, sleepy green eyes, huge
smooth brown thighs. She yawned and said,
"Less have a li'l love and a li'l nap, sweetie."

"Let me borrow a shower first."

"Sure. Sure, you go 'head. But hurry it up.
I'm in such a wonnerful mood, lover."

I went into the bathroom. It was a morass of
stale towels and sour swim suits, fetid and per-
fume-sweet, soapy and damp. It astonished me
not to find moss on the walls, mushrooms in
the corners, ferns behind the john. The stream
of water was feeble and tepid. I made the
shower last a long long time. I used the least
damp towel I could find. I opened the bathroom
door with great care, and as I had hoped and
expected, she was making a regular little
snare-drum snore, saying "Paah" with each exhalation. I dressed stealthily, tip-toed to the
bed, removed the black towel and tossed it into
the bathroom. I put my empty beer can on the
floor next to hers. In the living room I found a
post card and a pencil stub. I wrote, "Corry,
sweet: Even when you're half asleep, you're
marvelous. I'll be in touch, honey." I put it on

the bed on the far side of her and tiptoed out,
grinning like an idiot. Or like Dads.

But the grin had the feel of a suture. These
are the little losers in the bunny derby, but
they lose on a different route than the Mari-
annes, or the ones you see in the supermarket
on the nights when they double the green
stamps, coming in junk cars, plodding the
bright aisles, snarling at their cross sleepy
kids. Deeleen and Corry save wistfulness for
thoughts of the key clubs. They could be the
center fold in anybody's sex book. You have to
stay with the kicks. Age twenty and age
twenty-one. The cats always show up. The
phone always rings. Friends have friends. It
isn't like anything was going to wear out,
man. It isn't like they were going to stop having conventions. And you get a little tired or a
little smashed or a little bored, so you throw a
big fast busy fake and it is over in nothing at
all. And learn the ways to work them for the
little gifts here and there. Like maybe a
cruise. Or the rent. Or a couple beach outfits
by Cole. Friendship gifts. Not like you were
really working at it. The ones work at it, there
is always some character taking the money,
and there can be police trouble and all that.
You work waitress once in a while. The rest of
it is dates, really. One date at a time. And
some laughs, and if you're short, he can loan
you. And other numbers to call when there's a
whole bunch of guys.

This is the queasy shadowland, and they
don't even work hard at that because they
have never learned to work at anything. They
turn sloppy, and when the youngness is gone,
there isn't much left. Just the dead eyes and
the small meaty skills and the feeling their
luck went bad sometime, when they weren't
watching. Fifteen to twenty-five is the span,
and they age quickly and badly. These are the
bunnies who never find a burrow.

I got back to Lois in the hot blue dusk and
she was extraordinarily docile. She wore a
little navy blue dress with a starched white
collar, and she had her dark hair flattened to
severity. She gave the impression she was
dedicating her life to sobriety and good works.

I forgave her all indiscretions, and her dark
eyes glowed.

After dinner I told her about the cruise. I
told her what I planned to do. We went over
the plans, amending them, tightening them
here and there. We did not talk of the end of it,
even though the end was implicit in the things
that had to happen before the end.

She kissed me a good night with quick cool
lips, a dark glance that swiveled demurely
away.

In my bed I thought of the brutal leathery
hands of Junior Allen. Behind the agreeable
grin he was as uncompromising as a hammer.
Beast in his grin-mask. A clever, twisted
thing, hunting for that perversion of in-

nocence, the horrification of gentleness which would feed his own emptiness.

And I began thinking of that gentleness nearby. I computed the distance with care. Twenty-one feet, perhaps, from bed corner to bed corner. Would it not be good for her spirit, her morale, to be desired? Left alone, would she become dubious of her own time of a gentle aggression? And would not her fastidious litheness take away the heavy taste of the fleshy girls in the Citrus Inn? McGee, the Perfidious. Rationalizer. Womanizer. Gonadal argumentation. Go to sleep.

Was she on her left side? Her right side? Was she wakeful too? Were her eyes open in the same darkness, listening to the same whispery drone of the air conditioning? Was she wondering why I did not desire her?

Go to sleep, McGee, for God's sake. You want a permanent dependent?

I sat up. My heart was bumping and my breath was shallow. I went in there, moving as silently as a drift of smoke. She would be sleeping. I would turn right around and glide away from there.

I moved close to the bed, barely making out the dark spill of the pillowed hair, holding my breath to try to hear the cadence of her breathing. She made a small throaty sound of total contentment, of a perfect gladness, and reached and found my wrist and drew me to her, flipping the sheet and blanket aside,

presenting herself so totally, guiding us with
such an artful ease, that as I lay with her we
were joined, her readiness and her long exult-
ant shudder a confession of what her night
thoughts had been. After a few moments she
stilled us, so sweetly enclasped, saying, as she
turned us, "Wait, darling. Please. The way we
talked tonight. I could not really look at you.
You couldn't really look at me. Because we
couldn't say anything about the end of it. And
that's a shadow. You know it is."

"There isn't any other choice."

"You know there is. I can charge him with
rape. It's true enough, you know. I can testify.
They can put him away."

"It won't look very good for you. Staying
with him."

"Look good to whom? I care about my opinion of myself and your opinion of me. No one
else. He terrorized me. I'm articulate. I can
make anyone see how it was. And I can talk to
Cathy and she will identify him as the man
who beat her. Between the two of us, darling,
we can make certain he'll be put away for a
long time. Get the first part of it done, and before he can retaliate, we'll go to the police,
Cathy and I."

"I don't think that's the way to . . ."

"I want it that way. Promise."

"But . . ."

She had her fingers laced at the nape of my
neck. She gave me a hearty tug. "Promise!"

"You have me at a disadvantage."

"Ah, I have you at an advantage, McGee. Promise!"

". . . All right."

She pulled strongly. She rocked her wide mouth against my shoulder in a dainty, exacting, continuing, irresistible demand. And at last murmurously curled herself into sleep, the small love words falling away into heavy slumber. Once she was gone I had a little time to think of the promise. I looked at it coldly. It was a tactical stupidity. Junior Allen, once he was trapped, would spoil everything he could reach. He would try to make deals. And he would have the knowledge of Sergeant David Berry's fortune to bargain with, stolen, restolen, and stolen once again . . . if all went well for me.

Yet I knew I would keep the promise. Try to salvage something. She moaned in her sleep. Her long legs twitched. She was running from an old horror. I stroked her hair and kissed her eyes and she came half awake and sighed and settled back again.

If it all went wrong, would anyone ever be able to comfort Patty Devlan?

doce

THE small insured package from Harry arrived Monday morning. When I got back from the post office, Lois, excited and nervous, told me that Howard Wicker had called collect and left the message that the *Play Pen* was set up for a ten o'clock appointment Tuesday morning for installation of the new generator.

"It's moving so quickly," she said, wide-eyed.

I opened the package and took out the imitation gem. It was deep blue, big as a songbird's egg, with a bright and perfect star. I did a stupid thing. I bent and rolled it across the floor toward her. It rolled crookedly. Had it been a snake she could not have leapt back more violently, ashen and trembling, putting her hand to her throat, looking sick.

"Just like that," she whispered.

"Pick it up."

She hesitated a long moment, then reached and picked it up. Her color was coming back. She studied it and looked at me. "This really isn't real?"

"Not unless my friend made a horrible mistake."

"It's beautiful."

"Cornflower blue. Long ago they were thought to be love charms. It wouldn't fool an expert."

"Will it fool Junior Allen?"

"For just long enough, I think."

"My God, Trav, be careful!"

I took it away from her and wrapped it in some of the tissue from the small box and put it into my pocket.

She wore blue sailcloth shorts I had not seen before, a blouse with a narrow blue and white horizontal stripe. We had a connubial flavor this morning, but awkward. I had stayed the night with her, and when the early snarl of the fishermen leaving had awakened me, I had made love to her again. Without words. Afterward, she had rolled onto her stomach and wept, and could not say why and could not be soothed. She had showered first, and when I came out she was busy fixing breakfast, her mouth small, her face prim, her eyes evasive.

"What are you going to do?" I asked her.

"Just some lawyer things, about the sale of the house. It won't take long."

"Make it last. Keep busy. Keep your mind off this."

I offered her Miss Agnes, but she decided she would rather take a cab. She changed to a skirt and left. There is a cab stand up by the charter boat docks.

I looked at a chart and estimated that Junior Allen would cast off at about seven to be at Robinson-Rand by ten. With happy cruise passengers. Suddenly the careful plan seemed full of basic flaws. How could I be so certain he kept the loot aboard the *Play Pen*?

Logically, that was the best place for it. He was good with his hands. He'd had all the time in the world to prepare a hiding place. A forty-foot cruiser is a complex piece of equipment. It would take days to make a careful search of every inch of it. I'd had a good opportunity to study the layout, and saw no good reason why my short cut wouldn't work. If the random factors didn't get too random. If they didn't get out of control. He'd had more luck than he deserved.

And I had done my homework on him. Know the man, know the terrain, know the values. Nothing had been wasted and, I hoped, nothing overlooked.

There is as much danger in overestimating as in underestimating the quality of the opposition.

A. A. Allen, Junior, came through as a crafty, impulsive and lucky man. He had gone after the sergeant's fortune with guile and patience, but now that he had begun to have the use of it, he was recklessly impatient to find his own rather perverse gratifications. Sanity is not an absolute term. Probably, in the five years of imprisonment, what had originally been merely a strong sexual drive had been perverted into a search for victims. He had indulged himself with erotic fantasies of gentle women, force, terror, corruption. Until, finally, the restolen fortune became merely a means to that end, to come out and live the fantasies.

Cathy was a victim. And then Lois Atkinson. And Patty Devlan was next. As if each satisfaction required that the next victim be more vulnerable, more open to terror. Taste is quickly jaded. Make a projection of his trend and his needs, and it might well end up with the jump-rope set, and then become murderous because smaller mouths would not stay closed.

Good old Dads. Would honey like a nice boat ride on the nice man's boat? Would sweetie like a nice ten-day nightmare?

The five of them aboard would, catalyzed by a total isolation and the brute heat of the islands in August, and by the closeness of flesh in a confined space, by the liquor, by the meaty and casual permissiveness of the girls from the Citrus Inn, finally embark on those permutations and interrelations which would fit Junior Allen's fantasies. Good old Dads would gradually take charge, and all the fragile alarms of Miss Patty would find no response in the sun-dulled and drink-dulled paganism of Corry and Deeleen and Pete, find among them no protective conspiracy to save her from that inevitable result of Junior Allen's sly maneuvering, that obligatory scene for her when good old Dads would, smiling, and with grotesque ham-handed imitation of tenderness, gather her squeaking and whimpering and pleading into the seaman's bunk for that thickened and driving instruction, that hammering indoctrination which would thrust her quickly along the road of not giving a damn, not for Pete, not for herself, not for any of the abandoned and gentle dreams. Poor frantic little clown-girl, hiding the loveliness behind the heavy lenses, the shrill guffaw, the exaggerated gawkiness. Have some nice candy, sweetheart, and go with the nice man in his nice car, and wave goodby to all your friends.

I had made a note of the phone number in the Citrus Inn apartment, and I phoned. Deeleen answered. "Who? Oh sure. Hi. You want Corry? Well, she isn't here. You want her, what you do is call that bitch after I've gone."

"What's the matter?"

"I've had it with her, boy. Believe me, I've had it. You should have hung around. It was a big evening. She got drunk and she got nasty. I'm telling you, we're splitting up."

"Is the cruise off?"

"Hell no! We're leaving from here six-thirty

tomorrow morning, and go some place to get some work done on the boat and leave from there and go to Bimini at night. In the moonlight. Like I told her, the only thing I want is come back and find her moved out. She says I should move out. Where does she get that? I found this place, didn't I? Who needs her? She likes to spoil everything for everybody. The thing was, she snuck off with Pete. He's a nice kid, but what's the point? She knew he's been trying to make out with Patty for months, God knows why, but that's their business, isn't it. She had to know it would bitch up the cruise and all. It was a mess around here last night, Patty crying her eyes out. So she busted up the trip sort of, but she didn't spoil it. That's what we decided last night after she came back to the boat with Pete, both of them stoned, and there was a big fight and they took off. Just Dads and Patty and me. And the hell with Corry and Pete. I don't know where they are, and nobody cares. The cruise'll get Patty's mind off him. The thing is, there'd have been no harm done if Pete gets from her what Patty won't give him yet, but she has to come back smashed and bragging about it in front of Patty."

"How did it all start, Dee?"

"I don't know. We were all just kidding around, rough kidding maybe, and Corry got sore at something Dads said, and then Pete got sore at something Patty said to Corry, and then Corry went away, and a little while later Pete slipped away."

My admiration for Junior Allen was reluctant. He had simplified things for himself. They could not know that they had been maneuvered, any more than Cathy had known in the beginning. So he could set off with his little putty-haired pig, and with the wan victim of the lover's quarrel and the betrayal.

"I was going to stop around a little later on, Dee, and have a bon voyage drink with you people."

"There's nobody here now but me, Trav. Dads is off picking up supplies. Patty went home. She's coming back tonight and stay here at the apartment so we can get off at six-thirty like Dads wants. My stuff is aboard already, so I'll probably sleep aboard tonight. Maybe Patty too, if she wants. What you could do, you could come around tonight because four would be better'n three for a bon voyage drink?"

"You don't think Corry will be back?"

"Man, I *know* she won't be back. She and Pete took off together, and they're shacked someplace. She's out of the picture, Trav. You know, I wisht Patty was more of a doll, and then maybe you'd like to come along, because now there's room. What you do, when you come around, you take a good look at her. It could turn out three's a crowd and she'll need comforting the way she feels now. She's really got a nice complexion. And she says things you would laugh yourself sick when she's feeling good."

"That would be up to Dads."

"You can come around and if you like the idea, then we can ask him, but it wouldn't be fair not telling you you don't make out with Patty. She's got a thing about it, scared or something. I don't know. Maybe it would be different, off on a cruise. The way I figure it, if you want to go, honey, I can make Dads do about anything I want. Come right down to it, this cruise was my idea in the first place."

"I guess he can afford it."

"A guy like that, he gets what he wants and I get what I want, so it works out nice, and he wants to keep it that way. You come around later on, huh?"

"I'll be there."

"You don't have to bring any bottle, honey. Dads has loaded cases of it aboard."

My lady returned. Tilty eyes, swirl of a white skirt, little beads of the hotness on her upper lip and at her hairline.

I took her hands. Swung her around. "You are a fine fine thing."

"What's happened to you?"

"I like lovely ladies. You are refreshing."

"I'm hot and sticky."

"And rich?"

"I mailed the check to the bank." I beamed at her. She asked me again. "What's going on?"

"It's the contrast, I think. Because you can cry and not know why. Because I was looking around and saw your toothbrush. And some diaphanous items dripping dry in our shower stall. And because you have tidy hips, and when you are very passionate, it is all of you trying to say what your heart is saying, not just an end in itself—which sounds like a vulgar pun and isn't at all."

"Have you been drinking?"

"I'm drunk with power. Phantom McGee strikes again. Junior Allen is a stupid crafty man. And McGee is going to put him out of business."

She looked alarmed. "Darling, he's a terrible man."

"I am even more terrible in my wrath. How's this for glower?"

"Remarkable."

"No hairs in the sink and you put the butter away."

She looked owlish. "Are we engaged?"

"Ask me again, after we put this dull, foolish, sly fellow out of commission."

She swallowed. "We?"

"I need one very small assist from you."

She swallowed again. "And this act you're putting on is supposed to give me confidence?"

"Doesn't it?"

"Not very much."

"No danger for you."

"You know what just seeing him did to me."

"I know. Lois, he just isn't that ominous.

Evil, but not ominous. Sly, but not prescient. Once he is off balance, he will stay off balance, and fall heavily. And the law will gather him in."

She sat, her face wan and thoughtful. "What do you want me to do, Travis?"

In the sultry blue dusk, the three of us lounged in the spacious cockpit of the *Play Pen*, kindly old lump-jawed, crinkle-eyed Dads Allen in his spotless whites, Deeleen slumped and placid in low-waisted short shorts and a narrow halter which provided a startling uplift, Fearless McGee in pale blue denims and an old gray sport shirt. McGee with a short sturdy pry bar taped to his leg, and an old white silk sock in his pocket, with a goodly heft of bird shot knotted into the toe of it.

A lazy hour of the day. Deeleen yawned and said, "Patty should be along any time." She lazily scratched her belly, her nails making a whispering, fleshy, sensuous sound. "How about Trav coming along with us, lover?"

"I don't know whether I want to," I said.

Dee snickered. "He wants another look at Patty, huh?"

"We haven't invited him yet," Junior Allen said.

"What I want to do over there," Deeleen said, "I want me one of those buckets with the glass in the bottom, and you look at the coral and fish and stuff. And I want to go shopping in Nassau. Are you going to stake me for a little shopping, lover?"

"All you can use," he said, his smile white in the night. Lights were reflected on the still black water of the sea-walled canal. Two kinds of music merged in the softness of the night.

"Geez, I wish we could take off tonight, as soon as Patty gets here," she said.

"How is she going to get here?" I asked.

"She's taking a cab, like to go to the bus station, but she isn't," Dee said. She tilted her glass. The ice rattled up against her lips. I had been trying to time the drinks, and this time her glass and mine were empty, and Junior Allen's was more than half full. I stood up and reached and took her glass and said, "Okay if I fix a couple?"

"Go ahead," he said.

I went below. There was a light on in the galley. Spotless galley. Pristine whites. Trim happy ship. I gave her a heavy shot and hoped it would cover the other taste. Twisted the two capsules open, spilled the powder, stirred it in. A powerful barbiturate. Even with the liquor, I was more than reasonably sure it would do her no harm. She was a young and healthy animal. Fifteen minutes after she got it down, she would become unbearably sleepy. It would knock her out for a good fourteen hours, and leave her dulled and lethargic for the following two days. I wondered with a certain irony if it wasn't practically what Junior Allen had all planned for her, and I was merely jumping the gun. Or maybe he had decided she would be a willing accomplice.

I put no liquor in mine.

She murmured thanks when I gave her the drink. I had observed her drinking habits. One swallow at a time, one minute between swallows, until it all was gone. The taste seemed to suit her.

A breeze moved the cruiser, nudged it gently against a piling.

"She oughta be here pretty soon," Dee said. "If she doesn't come, the hell with her, lover. Who needs her?"

"She'll be along," Junior Allen said.

"Just the three of us, we could have a ball," Dee said. "She's not much of a swinging thing. Who needs her?" She yawned. "And she'll be drag-assin' around, crying over Pete anyways."

Dusk had deepened into night, and I saw the stars, and two planes winking, and heard the cheeing of the night insects mingled with the sound of music.

Deeleen yawned vastly and said, "I can't keep my eyes open. Lover, I'm going to go sack out for a while." She stood up heavily. She looked at him and made a kissing sound. As she passed me, she dragged her fingertips across my cheek. She went below, wobbling along the narrow area between the bunks as though the *Play Pen* were in a choppy sea. She bent and rolled herself heavily onto a bunk. From where I sat, I could see a narrow path of light from the galley light stretching diagonally across her, across the downy small of her back, the deep crease of her waist and the high gluteal round of her hip. Sweet dreams, sweet girl. Slide way way down. Stay out of the action.

I talked with Junior Allen. He didn't have his mind on it. He was crouched in the brush, and he could taste lamb, and he was alerted for the first shy sound of the little hoofs coming along the trail. I gently and indirectly advanced the idea of my coming along, and he firmly closed the door. He got up and sprang nimbly onto the dock, snapped the weak dock light on, checked his lines, adjusted a fender and came aboard again, restless.

Suddenly a man came onto the dock out of the shadows. He wore a gaudy shirt, wrinkled pants and a bright red fishing hat.

"Anybody here name of Mister Allen?" he asked in a soft voice.

"I'm Allen."

The man fumbled in his shirt pocket and took out a piece of paper. He squatted on the edge of the dock and held it out and said, "Apex Taxi, Mister Allen. You're to call the lady at this here number."

Junior Allen snatched it and turned it toward the light and looked at it. "What lady? She give this to you?"

"No, sir. I got called over the radio and put it down on that paper. They say come here and find you and give it to you." He straightened up and hesitated for a moment, and then went back the way he had come.

"Probably from Patty," I said.

It was the spur he needed. He hesitated, and I could sense that he was considering ordering me ashore and locking up, locking Deeleen on the inside. I slumped deeply in the canvas chair and said, "If it isn't her, and she should come while you're off phoning, I'll tell her you'll be right on back."

"You do that," he said. He sailed up onto the dock and went off. He had a springy and muscular gait, like a Percheron in a spring pasture.

I counted to ten and then went below. I found the lights and turned them on. I went through that boat like a nervous whirlwind, yanking out the drawers and dumping them, pawing through stowage areas. I had little hope of finding a thing, but I wanted it to look like a thorough search. And as I yanked and scurried and spilled, I was pleading with Lois. "Keep him going, baby. Keep him hanging on the line. Keep him hooked." We had planned some interesting things to say to the monster. In spite of the racket I was making, Deeleen did not make a quiver.

I selected a spot very carefully, a lighted place where his glance would fall naturally, and I placed the fake sapphire precisely, right where it could have fallen from the hand of a hasty thief. I put a fifty-dollar bill on the cockpit deck where the interior lights shone out upon it. I turned the dock light out and snapped the switch off, breaking it. Then I clambered quickly to the cabin roof and flattened myself out on the far side of the dinghy. I checked my observation points. I could hold onto the safety rail and lean over and look through the port into the small forward cabin, or hitch back a few feet and look the same way into the larger cabin.

I thought I knew exactly what he would do, what he had to do under those circumstances. Lois had been very dubious about this part. And she had been worried about somebody coming along. But she had been wrong there, and would be wrong again, I knew.

I heard his hasty footsteps on the dock. I kept my head down. I heard the thump and felt it as he leaped down into the cockpit. I heard his grunt of consternation.

He would have to find out, and find out quickly. I leaned over cautiously and stared in, my head upside down. I saw him snatch the gem up, stare at it, shove it into his pocket. He whirled toward his marine radio rig, grasped the wooden drawer directly under the rig and pulled it all the way out. A strange resonant buzzing began. He reached back in the place where the drawer had been, and the buzzing stopped. He worked at something in there, and then pulled his arms out, a cloth bag in one hand and a small plastic bag of paper money in the other. He examined them. He stowed them away again, started the buzzer and replaced the drawer. As soon as the drawer was in place, the buzzing sound stopped. He went to the sleeping girl. He took her brutally by the hair, lifted her and wrenched her around. His back was to me. It was a very broad back. Her eyes opened, wide and absolutely vacant, and she seemed to stare so directly at me, I almost yanked myself away from the port. She closed her eyes again. He slapped her. They stayed close. He dropped her.

Suddenly he reached into his pocket and took out the stone. He moved closer to the nearest light. His body seemed to tense, shoulders lifting. I pulled myself back up, sensing that he would whirl, that he would catch me.

I wormed my way toward the stern, onto the overhang, working the silk sock out of my pocket. The lights below began to go off quickly, one after the other. I had not counted on that. I closed my eyes tightly for several seconds and then opened them wide, trying to hurry night vision. I heard him coming. Moving swiftly. I wanted one good chance, and I had to take a risk to get it. I slid head and shoulders over the edge as he came out. He heard or sensed the movement and tried to turn, but I got him very nicely and solidly, better than I had expected. He took three wandering sideways steps and went down onto his hands and knees. I dropped, landing on toes and knuckles, and as he straightened, I gave it to him with more precision, more of a wrist-snapping impact. He went back down

onto his hands, shaking his head, sighing. I
marveled at the toughness of his skull. I
snapped him behind the left ear and his arms
quit and his face smacked the teak deck. For a
moment, standing and breathing hard, I
debated lashing him up. But after three of
those, I guessed he would last more than long
enough for my two chores, finding and taking
his treasures, and disabling his boat.

The drawer arrangement was tricky. He had
a battery buzzer back in there. I couldn't find
his manual switch, so I yanked the wires loose.
The compartment was directly behind the
drawer, with a sliding lid. I shoved the money
into one pocket. I jounced the cloth sack. It
made a glassy clinking sound. It stirred an old
memory. Glassies won in the school-yard long
ago, a heft marking many victories. I shoved
the sack inside my shirt. They had a strange
collness through the cloth against my skin. A
Himalayan coolness perhaps, cold as smuggled
gold. Or cell bars. Or those small blue eyes
above the lovable smile.

The boat would be no problem. Hoist a
hatch, tear off a handful of wiring. But then I
remembered the fake stone. If I couldn't send
it back, Harry would want a lot more than it
was worth. I squatted beside Junior Allen and
felt it in his right trouser pocket. I worked my
hand into the pocket. Suddenly he rolled
against my hand, pinning it, rolled onto my
wrist and arm and the leverage forced me
down against the deck. Then he was on his

back, my right arm under him. He hooked his
left arm around my neck, pulled my head
against his waist and began hammering me
with his free hand. I had no leverage and no
room to strike back. As my face began to
break, and the world began to blur, I planted
my knees and stuffed my other arm under him
and heaved. It brought him up and turned
him, and I ripped my right hand free of his
pocket. He bounded up with a rubbery agility,
and I barely saw the kick coming, and turned
just enough to take it on the point of the shoulder. My left arm went numb. He was a jolly
brawler. He kept low and balanced, snorting
with each exhalation, and I hit him twice before he bowled me over and bore me down in a
tangle of chairs and began the jolly business of
rib cracking, gouging, kneeing and breaking
everything loose he could reach. He clambered
and straddled me, trapping my arms under his
blocky legs, picked me up by the ears and
banged my head back onto the teak. As the
world went slow and dreamy, I got an arm
loose and saw my hand way up there, the heel
of it under his chin. He tried to hammer his
clasped hands down onto my rigid arm, and
would have snapped it nicely had I not gotten
my feet braced and bucked him off. He was
back at me like a cat, and he swung a hard
chunk of wood from one of the smashed chairs.
I caught the first one on the shoulder and I
cleverly caught the next one right over the left
ear. It broke a big white bell in my head, and he

side-stepped, grunting for breath, and let me go down. I landed on my side, and he punted me in the belly like Groza trying for one from the midfield stripe.

I had that fractional part of consciousness left which gave me a remote and unimportant view of reality. The world was a television set at the other end of a dark auditorium, with blurred sound and a fringe area picture. Somewhere the happy smiler leaned against the rail and sucked air for a time. I couldn't have fluttered an eyelid if somebody had set me on fire. He began cleaning up the cockpit. He hummed to himself. I recognized the tune. "Love is a Many Splendored Thing." William Holden and Jennifer Jones. I remembered her going into the shallows of that bay in Hong Kong in that white swim suit. But I couldn't keep my mind on her. Every time Dads got in range of me, he kicked. In time to the music. Then he kicked me in the head. It faded that distant television set right out, right down to a little white dot and then that was gone too. . . .

. . . The little set came back to life. There was vibration. Marine rumble. Sound of the wake. Boat idling along. And a thin and hopeless little female voice nearby saying, "Oh, don't. Oh, don't any more. Oh, please don't any more please."

I was folded into a corner of the stern of the cockpit. I had to puzzle that voice out. Slowly.

Dear little Patty. But she wasn't supposed to be around. I'd written her out of the script. And Junior went, "Ho, ho, ho." Like a jolly Santa. "You are a cute little ole button," he said. "You're a tasty bit."

I picked one eye and pumped it open. Right eye. It was like jacking up a truck. In the night radiance, Junior Allen was ho-ho-hoing Miss Patricia Devlan. He was crouched at her like a bear, and he had her butted back against the transom, both her thin wrists held behind her in one hand, and his other hand up under her skirt, lifting her onto tiptoe. They were close enough to fall on me.

Suddenly he turned and stared forward and grunted, released her and went up toward the wheel. A course correction, reset the automatic pilot, came back to the fun. But I did not want anyone ho-ho-hoing Miss Devlan. She was hunched over, sobbing. I came up with blinding speed—like one of those trick clothes drying racks being unfolded by a sleepy drunk. I was forty feet tall and one inch wide, with a head fashioned of stale gas. As Junior roared, I slooped one dead arm out and around the girl's waist, pulled her toward me and rocked right over backward with her, over the rail and down into the black bay water, tucking in all elbows and knees, feeling the wrench of the water, waiting to see how a prop would feel chopping meat.

We popped up in the turbulence, and I saw the running lights receding at a comforting pace. I looked around at shore lights, orienting myself. We were about one mile south of the kick in the head, in a place where the bay was wide, but the channel was fairly narrow. She tilted her pale child-face back, her hair pasted seal black to her head, and made a waffling sound of total hysteria. The boat stopped bubbling along and roared into a turn. I clopped Miss Devlan across the chops and shoved her in the best direction and yelled, "Swim, baby!"

She came out of it. She swam very well indeed. She pulled ahead of me. I felt as if I were swimming with four broken arms. And with each breath I could convince myself he was still kicking me in the stomach. We had a good angle of escape. We had to go fifty feet to get past the submerged spoil banks from the channel dredging. He had to come back about a hundred and fifty yards. I was hoping I could sucker him into jamming it aground. But I heard him throttle down sharply, then roar the engines again as he put it into reverse to sit dead in the water.

"Keeping going," I yelled at her. "Angle a little left."

The spotlight hit us. She stopped swimming. I took two big strokes and reached her and bore her under. Pistols make a silly spatting sound over open water. And slugs hitting near you make a strange sound. *Tzzeee-unk*. *Tzzeee-unk*. I tried to kick us along and she got the idea. The underwater breast stroke felt as if it pulled my ribs free of my breastbone. I lost her. I grabbed some air and went down again and kept churning along. I peered up and saw no radiance, and came up and looked back. He was in a big curve, and he straightened out and went ramming south toward Lauderdale.

"Patty?" I yelled.

"H-here I am," she said, about ten feet behind me. She was standing in waist-deep water. I went to her and felt the lumpy edges of an oyster bar underfoot.

"He . . . He . . . He was going to . . ."

"But he didn't."

"He . . . He . . . He was going to . . ."

"He's gone. Pull yourself together."

I put an arm around her. She leaned her face against my chest and said, "Haw! Oh God. Haw!"

"Come on, baby."

"I'm . . . I'm all right. He took my glasses off and threw them overboard. He said I'd never need them again. I c-can't hardly see without them."

"He's gone, Patty. And he's got his little chum with him, and they deserve each other. Get yourself collected, and then we'll swim to shore." Behind her, two hundred yards away, was the bright shore, loud with neon in the night. It made pink and green and blue highlights on her hair. I let her go. Her blouse was pasted to her peach-sized breasts. Except for the breasts, she looked about twelve. With them, she looked fourteen.

"How did you get into the act?" I asked her.

"I phoned your mother and told her the damn fool thing you were planning to do."

"That was you? I . . . I went out my bedroom window. I didn't want to . . . miss the fun."

"He's a real fun fellow, old Dads is."

"Don't, please. He said I was the one he was really after. I went to the boat and everything was . . . so strange. You were lying there so still and bloody I thought you were dead. He told me to go below and wake Dee up. I tried, and I couldn't. I wanted to go home then. He said we were going to have a nice cruise, not to worry. He said you'd tried to rob him. He said he was going to turn you over to the police. He said you were just knocked out. He said that before he turned you in, he wanted to get your accomplice too. He told me to stay aboard and watch you, and give a yell if you woke up. He said he'd be hiding close by. I didn't like it, but I stayed there like he said. I was thinking about Pete and that girl, and I just didn't care what I did. Then a woman came. A tall pretty woman. She stood on the dock and she said in a loud voice, 'What have you people done to him? What have you done to Travis McGee?' She couldn't see you from there."

"Dear God! She was waiting for me in my car. She should have run when she knew something had gone wrong."

"He came out of nowhere and swooped her right up and jumped aboard with her. She started to scream and then she saw you and stopped. He let go of her and she just stood there,

staring at you. While she wasn't moving . . . he
. . . he hit her. With his fist. It was such a terrible
blow it made me sick to my stomach. She fell like
a rag doll and he picked her up and put her in a
bunk. I got off. But he caught me and brought me
back. He threw the lines off and started up.
When he got out of that little canal he went real
fast out to the main channel and real fast for a
little while south down the channel, then he
slowed it down and fixed it to steer itself and
came back and threw my glasses away and
started . . . doing things to me. I guess . . . I could
have jumped overboard. But I couldn't think of
anything . . . and then you . . ."

"Come on! Can you make it now? Come on,
girl!"

We swam side by side. It all seemed so
damned slow. I headed for the brightest
clustering of lights. We ended up in the shells
and shallows at the base of a five-foot sea wall.
I got the top of it and wormed my way over it,
reached down and got her wrists and yanked
her up. She stumbled and fell into the damp
night grass at the base of a coconut palm. I
picked her up and herded her along with me,
our rubber shoes squelching, breaths wheez-
ing, strides unsteady. I had to get to a phone.
My face felt like a multiple fracture. I steered
us around a rock garden before we fell into it.
It was a motel complex, and for reasons which
defy the imagination it was named The Bearpath. They were doing a nice little summer

business. The dance instructors were Bossa-Novaing a clutch of tourists, all of whom looked as if they did each other's hair for a living. Bidding was vicious in the cardroom. We came churning in, dripping and battered and winded.

Dapper little fellows came running toward us, wringing their hands, making shrill little cries of consternation.

"Phone!" I demanded.

"But you can't come in here like this . . ."

I grabbed the nearest handful of silk blazer and lifted it onto its tippy toes, and he pointed a rigid arm at a salmon phone on a baby blue counter. When I asked the switchboard girl to get me the County Sheriff's office, she asked in a voice wet with acid and post-nasal drip if I was a guest of the hotel. I told her that if she delayed the call one more second, I would start throwing their guests through their window walls, as a gesture of impatience. Patty stood docile beside me, chin down, shoulders rounded, and her little rump tucked humly under.

I got a deputy who was so bright and so quick it helped me pull myself together. I was aware of all the silence behind me, the stilled dancers, the frozen card games, the fellows in pastel silk. I described the boat. I said it had left the Citrus Inn maybe forty minutes ago, and was headed south, A. A. Allen, Junior, possibly psycho, in command. Young girl aboard, drugged and unconscious. Deeleen.

Last name unknown. And a Mrs. Lois Atkinson, taken aboard against her will, and slugged. May plan to head out from Lauderdale to the Bahamas.

"What's your name and where are you calling from?"

"The Bearpath Motel. I have a girl who needs attention, and needs to be taken home. A Miss Devlan . . ."

"We have an alert on a Patricia Devlan, eighteen, dark hair, slender build . . ."

"The same. In her case it was attempted kidnapping and attempted assault. You can pick her up here."

"What's your name?"

I hung up and gave a brief glance at the forty or fifty pairs of bulging eyeballs, and turned and found a way out. I went through some hedges and a flower bed and a parking lot. I had a vivid little silvery grinding in my chest with each breath. I headed toward commercial lights and oriented myself. Better than a mile back to Miss Agnes. Scout pace, they call it. Run fifty steps, walk fifty. The car was there. No key. But the spare was up under the dash in a little magnetic box.

I headed her for home. I heard myself sob. It was like a big hiccup. A sad brave wonderful gal who had trusted me. She'd trusted me. She'd trusted reliable old McGee. They had to stop trusting me. Damn them for trusting me. I blinked and drove and cursed McGee.

trece

A dry shirt and pants made no remarkable improvement in my appearance. I trudged to the huge neighboring cruiser where my joyous friend, the Alabama Tiger, operates the world's only permanent floating house party. He had some hundred proof for immediate medication, asked me who had dragged me down a flight of stairs by the heels, and offered me the temporary loan of my choice among several eager amateur nurses. But I told him I would rather borrow the *Rut Cry*. He didn't ask why. He told me to take it. He likes to get up and fly. The *Rut Cry* is twenty-one feet of white water hull with big tanks and two big Mercs astern. It was moored alongside, gassed and ready. A chattering flock of the Tiger's girls helped me strip the weather canvas off it, and handled the lines and shoved me off, the fast motors burbling; then they stood and waved me their musical goodbys. I belted myself down into the foam rubber seat, found the switch for the running lights, spun the boat and took it out and down, under the bridge, past the Navy and on out into the Atlantic. Once clear of the channel chop, I figured a rough heading for Bimini and let it go. At forty it began leaping clear, banging my teeth, collapsing my spine, cavitating, slamming, roaring. It was punishment for past sins, sticking knives in every bruise. Once I put a bow corner under and came too close to tripping it over. I pulled it back down to thirty. When I was well clear of any possible traffic, I cut the running lights. Southeast wind. No chop in the Stream. Big long ones I could take on the quarter. I estimated his hull would give him a cruising speed of fifteen tops. I could run in one hour what he could run in two. So give him a two-hour head start, right at the sea buoy. No. Make it an hour and a half from that point. And I had cleared it at nine-fifteen. So at nine-fifteen I was twenty-two miles behind him. Forty-five minutes. Give him another ten miles by the time I got to that point. Twenty minutes more. By rough reckoning, if all the guesses were right, I could run up on him by ten-thirty.

So I ran until ten-thirty, then cut to dead slow and headed directly into the long shallows swells. I undid the two straps and stood up, my hand braced on the top of the wheel. Each time I was at the crest of a wave, I tried to sweep one segment of the horizon. Moonlight silvered the spill of water. I was too far off to pick up the Cat Cay light. My heart jumped when I saw lights east and north of my position, but after three good looks at them, I knew it was a southbound freighter staying clear of the Stream. I stared until I began to see things that weren't there.

I sat down again and leaned my forehead against the top of the wheel. My tongue found an unfamiliar place where a corner of a tooth was gone. The valiant slob. Goof McGee. This was like trying to fill a straight with a three-card draw. He could run without lights too. He was too canny to head this way. He had enough range for Cuba. Or he knew a nice little corner he could tuck it into, down near Candle Key.

The irony of the stars looked down at my grandstand play and dwindled me. One man in one small boat in the vasty night. In my despair I let the boat swing and a small wave broke and slapped and sprayed my face. Tears and sea water taste much the same.

The authorities wouldn't stoop to the idiocy of a night search. They would wait for dawn and bring the choppers out, along with some playmates from the C.A.P. And some of the reserve boys needing flight time.

Suddenly the silver was gone. I looked up and saw a haloed thunderhead obscuring the moon. There was lightning under it, low and blue against the sea. So I began my run back, taking it slow, taking the bad motion of the sea on the stern quarter, climbing the long slow hills and then scooting down the other side. I looked toward the storm. I could outrun it by giving myself a beating. I had a rough heading home. It didn't have to be on the nose. It's a big coast. Hardly anyone ever misses it. When you come in at night you pick out the huge pink haze of Miami and then adjust your course accordingly.

The lightning was almost continuous. And as I looked toward it, I picked up something out of the corner of my eye. Some sort of blob between me and the lightning. I thought I had imagined it, and then I saw it again. I spun and headed toward it. It was gone and then I picked it up again. No lights. Just an outline against lightning in the darkening night. I soon had it again, larger, too big to miss. I made a big swing to come up astern. The next flash of lightning was close and bright, bright enough to give me the after-image of the pale cruiser on the black sea.

The *Play Pen*, slower than I thought, way behind the estimated schedule, and picked up by a freak of light and vision.

I hung back off his stern quarter and adjusted my speed to his. I lay about two hundred yards off. He was between me and the storm. There was little chance he would pick me up unless he happened to be looking in that direction when the next bright flash occurred. He was doing ten knots, possibly to conserve fuel, and according to my compass, he was on a heading that would bring him in well south of Bimini. It seemed possible he might figure on getting inside, in on the Bahama Bank and dropping the hook, and then heading on for the Berry Islands at first light. Get his fuel at Frazier's Hog Cay, a good reach for him, but possible.

It made a nice problem. I couldn't run up on him without him hearing the snarl of the Mercs. Shoved into my belt was the little Czech automatic I had picked up when I had changed clothes. It would fire every time, with a little bit more accuracy than a garden hose. And at the moment of trying to get aboard, I would be very vulnerable.

There was a click of blinding lightning, an ozone stink, a hard slam of thunder; I heard the hiss of the rain coming, and suddenly it moved across him and he was gone. It came drenching down on me, and I turned toward him, giving it a little more speed, straining to see him. Suddenly the stern loomed up in the rain. I spun the wheel and reversed both motors and narrowly avoided slamming into him. I could ask for no better cover than the rain, than the sound and the blinding screen of it. He moved on, and I hurried after him, risked leaving the wheel and scrambled forward and made it fast to the bow cleat. I hurried back and came back on course, and held the other end of the line in my teeth. He was pulling a big mound of water behind him, but I felt that if I could slide past that, there was relatively flat water alongside of him. The rain felt as solid as hail, and it was surprisingly cold. Squinting ahead, I made two false starts, and then ran it up just where I wanted it. I killed the motors, leaped and caught the rail. And felt the little pistol slid down my pant leg and rap the top of my foot. But it was too late to change my mind. As I went over the rail, I saw him hunched at the wheel in the next gleam of lightning. I took a quick turn of the line around the rail an instant before the dead weight of the *Rut Cry* came against it. The line did not pop, as I half expected. It felt like half-inch nylon. I made it fast. I squatted low and looked for Junior Allen. The lightning came. He was gone. The wheel was turning.

Without warning, the drenching rain stopped. The *Play Pen* had begun to turn in a big circle to port, rolling badly when it entered the trough. I glanced over my shoulder. The *Rut Cry* was plainly visible, riding well, nose high on the hump of water the cruiser was dragging. And the damned moon came out. I was a black bug in a bright silver box. Something snapped twice. A finger flicked at my hair, a bee whirred by my ear. I rolled into the far corner of the cockpit. My hand landed upon the haft of a boat hook. I yanked it out of the clips, half rolled and hurled it like a spear at the dark entrance to the cabin. There was a grunt and clatter and a soft curse. Then both engines slowed and chuckled and died and we lay dead in the water. The *Rut Cry* moved up and nudged the stern. We rocked. Gear creaked and rattled. I snatched up a chair we hadn't smashed during the earlier game, hurled it toward the darkness where I thought he was, and grasped the overhang of trunk cabin roof and swung myself up and crawled forward. I was in the open and in white moonlight, but he couldn't get to me without my seeing him.

The rain wind had moved the open boat out to the side, starboard, amidships, at the end of the nylon line. Holiday boat. Play pretty for the Tiger. I flattened myself out beside the overturned Fiberglas dinghy and, by touch, loosened the lashings which held it fast. I had no great plan. I wanted to create some more variables, trusting I could use them to my advantage. I wondered why he was so silent. It was unnerving. He had whipped me once, and I knew how brutally quick and strong he was. And I was not in as good shape as the last time. I could not recall doing him very much damage. But I couldn't let it come out the same way again. Not and live. I had made the mistake of thinking of him as a man, rather than an animal. He wasn't even a furry animal. He was reptilian. He had to be planning something.

Suddenly I realized that the *Rut Cry* was gliding slowly toward the cruiser. I inched forward and looked, and saw him bringing it in, a squat dark shape in the cockpit, outlined by the pale moonlight. He swung and snapped and as I yanked back like a turtle, a slug whined off the aerial into the night. Suddenly I realized what he could have been doing during all that silence. He could have been grabbing the wad of bills and a bag of marbles out of his hidey hole. I had come out of nowhere bearing the gift of a small fast boat and, presumably, enough gas to get back to the mainland. So *adios, compadre.* It made a nice solution for him. He would know that I had gotten away, and things were going very sour for him. He could right it very neatly. He could head for a dark piece of the mainland, set the boat adrift, and live to play other games in other places. I could do him no more harm than I had already done. It would not matter to him whether he left me dead or alive aboard the *Play Pen.* Once he freed the line and dropped into the *Rut Cry*, his chances were damned good. I couldn't catch him.

I waited just as long as I dared. The *Play Pen* was in the trough, rocking and thrashing, taking white buckets of water into the cockpit whenever a crest hit the port side as it was rolling that way. It was a so-called self-bailing cockpit, which merely means that the cockpit deck is higher than the normal waterline, and the water runs on out the scuppers set low into the transom corners.

When the *Rut Cry* was alongside and had been there for about five seconds, I put my hands under the bow of the overturned dinghy and flipped it up and over and down into the cockpit, and went after it. It made a great *brong* and *boomp*, and came bouncing up off the teak, giving him a glancing blow as it leaped out over the stern. It knocked him sprawling, and he dropped the coiled line from the *Rut Cry*. The line began to play out rapidly, as the wind, more effective in moving that hull than the hull of the bigger boat, began to push it off and away on the starboard side. I landed off balance, and timed the roll, and as he came up, I fell toward him, snapped both hands down onto the gun wrist as his arm started to swing around, and, against its resistance, went right on over it, clamping it, curling tight, like a kid doing a trick on a tree limb. I smacked the crown of my head onto the teak, legs swinging over, and felt something give in that arm just as I had to release it. We spilled into the tangled heap, awash in the stern starboard corner, both fighting to get loose. He went clawing and scrabbling after the end of the line as it moved on out over the starboard rail, and came within frantic reaching inches of it just before a wild roll to port rocked him back. In the moonlight I saw the white end of it yanked over the rail and off into the night as we rolled away from the slow pull of the drifting *Rut Cry*. I was kneeling, patting around in the water, reaching and feeling for the gun. His hands were empty, and I wondered if it had flipped overboard. He skidded on the seat of his pants, and for a moment the roll held him nailed against the port side. Water smashed in on him. I knew that he knew what he had to do. He had to take care of me and get the *Play Pen* moving and go downwind and get the smaller boat. I was the problem. My fingertips brushed the gun and I grabbed at it just as he used the roll to starboard to come at me. If he had come crawling he would have made it in time. But he got onto his feet to drive at me, and it gave me time to bring the gun up and fire once into his leathery paunch, and yank the trigger twice more without effect before he got his hands on me. He had begun a strange screaming, a whistling sound with each exhalation. It was not pain or fear. It was just a violent exasperation. If he was trying to stomp something that wouldn't lie still enough, he might make that same sound.

He grabbed me around the neck, but as I broke out of it, I realized the strength of his right arm was gone. He could use it, but it did not have that sickening power in it. I scuttled away from him and we were braced on hands and knees, nose to nose. The motion was too violent to risk standing up. We could not guard against each other. I had lost the gun.

He used his left hand. I used my right. We traded blows as they do in cheap television, groaning with effort, a measured grunt-smack, grunt-smack, grunt-smack. I knew that if I could keep it up, time was on my side. He had a bullet in him. Probably he realized he was losing ground. I saw him reach his left hand into the front of his shirt. Another gun? A knife? In sudden fright, I tried to hit him hard enough to finish it, but he yanked his head back, cat-quick, and I missed and sprawled flat. As I rolled, I saw him bringing something down at my head, and I yanked away. It struck me a glancing blow and hit the teak deck and burst. Then there were all the jelly beans, rolling and spilling, scattering and fleeing in the moonlight, the bright treasure from the cloth sack. He gave a howl of dismay and began scrambling, pouncing, snatching at the round gem stones. Water smashed in, sweeping them inevitably toward the stern, out the scuppers, seeding the deep with riches. I think he forgot for a moment that he had to do something about me. I got low, as I had been taught, and timed the roll, and as he lifted up a little too far, I drove at him, shoulder into the pit of the belly, legs driving. I drove him back into the starboard rail as it dipped low, and he went over, grabbing at me, clawing at me. But I got hold of the rail and he missed it and went into the sea.

I don't know why I expected him to go down like a stone. I clung to the rail, gasping and gagging, and saw him pop up, snap the water out of his eyes, orient himself, and turn and start churning his way toward the *Rut Cry*. With a sprained arm, with a bullet in his gut, I could still believe he would make it. It was out there, rising and falling in the moonlight.

In a strange kind of panic, I groped for something to throw at him. The *Play Pen* was drifting in the same direction. He was not getting out of range very fast. There was a big Danforth anchor in the open storage locked in the center of the transom. I pulled it out, chain rattling on the shaft, got the shaft in both hands, braced myself, threw it out there as hard as I could in a high clanking arc. It landed on the back of his head and neck and shoulders just as a wave lifted him, and tumbled forward over his shoulder—and the sea was suddenly empty. The line which had been bent onto the chain whipped at my ankle. By instinct I stepped on it. I bent weakly and picked it up. I didn't have the strength to pull the anchor back in. I gave it a couple of turns around the starboard stern cleat. I kept looking for him. I couldn't believe that anything had ended him. I took a step to catch my balance, and stepped on something like a pebble. I picked it up and put it in my pocket. I pulled myself to the controls. I had to stop all that damned motion before I went out of my mind. I got the engines started, turned it into the wind and put it on dead slow, and jacked the Metal Marine pilot into gear. It took over the wheel, holding it there. My underlip was in two segments, and one was folded down, exposing my teeth on the left side. I put the running lights on. There was a flashlight in a bracket beside the instrument panel. I went below. The violent motion had spilled both women out of the bunks. They lay in the narrow aisle, both face down, Deeleen atop Lois. I heaved Deeleen back up onto the port bunk. She was deep in her sleep, long exhalations rattling in her throat.

I was gentler with Lois, kneeling, turning her, gathering her up. I put the light on her when she was on the bunk. Her face was the color of yeast. Her lips were blue and bloodless. The whole left side of her face was a dark bruise. I could not detect respiration, but when I lay my ear against her chest I thought I could hear a thin, small, slow sound, a thready struggle of the heart.

I covered them both with blankets, tucking them around their bodies, muttering to myself. My head seemed full of distances, of wraiths and mists, a wide and lonely country encased in a papery fragility of bone.

Find the Tiger's boat. Priority one. Look downwind. I went to the controls and took it out of pilot and swung it to take the sea dead astern, and stepped it up a little. Suddenly I remembered the damned anchor. I wasn't tracking well. It would be very clever to wind the line around a shaft. A towed anchor will swing up and bobble around in the wake. I put it back on pilot and went astern. I decided I would just release the line and let it go. I put the light back into the wake to see if I could see it. The wake made a smooth hump about forty feet back of the transom. Junior Allen rode that hump, face up out of the water, grinning at me.

Suddenly, as if to show off, as if to prove how well he had everything under control, he made a complete roll, exposing the metallic gleam of the anchor for an instant, then steadying again, face high, making little white bow waves that shot past his ears.

I could not move or think or speak. The known world was gone, and in nightmare I fought something that could never be whipped. I could not take the light off him. He rolled again. And then I saw what it was. His throat was wedged in that space between the flukes of the Danforth, and the edges of the points were angled up behind the corners of his jaw, the tension spreading his jowls into that grin. I got to the cleat, and with nerveless stumbling hands I freed the line. He disappeared at once as the anchor took him down. I hugged the rail and vomited. When I looked forward, eyes streaming, I suddenly saw I was coming too damned close to running the *Rut Cry* down. I sprang to the controls, circled it, came up on it slowly, got its line with a boat hook and made it fast to the center cleat in the transom.

I made an estimate of the course, guessed it at two-ninety, and, watching the *Rut Cry* to see how it rode, I slowly put it up at 2800 rpm. I went down and looked at the women. Lois's hands were limp and icy. I found a pulse in her throat with my lips. She was alive.

I turned on the ship-to-shore and transmitted on the Coast Guard emergency frequency. On my third try they came in loud and clear. I told them who I was and where I was, and something of the nature of the medical emergency. It was after midnight. My lip made my voice strange. I told them I did not think from the looks of the woman and the sea a copter pickup was feasible. They told me to stand by. They came back on, and at their request, I took the flashlight and lifted her eyelids and looked at her eyes. I told them one pupil was tiny and the other was very large. They told me to stand by again. I went topside to look around. I saw a glow of lights on the western horizon. I swung the flashlight beam around and spotted a little red gleam in the scupper. I picked it up. I found three more after that. Five all told, the only ones which hadn't been washed into the sea.

They came back on and gave me a five-degree course correction, having spotted me in some mysterious way, and told me to make all possible speed for Lauderdale, and come right to the Pier 66 gas dock where an ambulance would be waiting.

I gave it all it would take. The marine engines roared. At full throttle they turned close to 4500. I backed them off a little. The tanks were half full, I slammed toward home, steering it by hand, the Tiger's boat wallowing and swinging astern.

Red lights were revolving and blinking on the shiny vehicles parked at the gas dock. I laid it in close and a gang of people swarmed aboard with lines, yelling orders to each other. They came aboard and took the women off, giving them an equally gentle professional handling.

I rode to the hospital with them. They stitched my mouth, X-rayed me, taped my ribs, eased my nose back to a reasonably central position. While they were doing that to me, other people shaved her head and cut into her skull and released the cumulative pressure of the massive cerebral hemorrhage. The operation was a great success. Three days later the patient died of pneumonia, under oxygen, with me sitting there, staring at her through the Pliofilm, willing every struggling breath she took, until finally she just did not take the next one. She settled smaller then, her face little and gray under the turban of gauze and adhesive.

catorce

WHAT do you do when they turn all your lights out?

I guess you answer the questions. There were a lot of people and a lot of questions, because it was what they call an interesting problem of jurisdiction.

And though you do not really give a damn how much or how little you tell them, there is, after all, an instinctive caution which takes over and tends to simplify the answers you give. I had no idea where he had gotten his money. Cathy had no idea either. She just thought he might possibly be the same man who had beaten her up. I was her friend. I was just trying to check it out, and had gotten

243

caught in the middle. And had had some luck.

Deeleen was as angry as a boiled squirrel for having slept through all the action. Patty made a resolute witness, precise, outraged and articulate.

I had a simple little story and told it forty times. Yes sir, I was pretty silly trying to find him in the dark out there in the ocean. He let me come aboard and then knocked me out. I was getting up when he was trying to climb into the other boat. I saw him lose his balance and fall in. I saw him swimming, trying to catch the other boat, but it was drifting as fast as he could swim. I was too weak and dizzy to do anything. I think I heard him call out once. I got the big boat started and I went looking for him, but when I found the other boat, it was empty.

I soon created a massive disinterest on the part of the reporters. I talked very freely and at great length. I could do twenty minutes on the characteristics of the *Play Pen*, and another twenty on the hull design of the *Rut Cry*. I could give an hour lecture on setting compensated compass courses, and what the weather had been like out there. They listened until their eyes glazed and their jaws creaked when they yawned. I did not tell them of my night visions of Junior Allen down there, his neck wedged into the anchor, his heels high, dancing slowly in vagrant currents.

There are some other things you do when they turn your lights out.

You learn how to use the darkness. Varieties of darkness. The darkness of hot sun on the beach, and intense physical effort. The small darkness of liquor. The small darkness of the Tiger's girls. But these do not work in any lasting way. The body mends, but a part of it took its last breath behind that glassine barrier.

Once in a while they show up to ask some more questions, but you are amiable, slightly stupid, and very polite. The sister-in-law had come down and gathered up what was left of the lady and had taken the remains north, for suitable burial in the family plot.

One day I realized I was nearly broke. And I had gone into this thing for the money. It was to laugh. Somewhere behind my heart I thought I heard her small amusement, a faint melody. Who are we laughing at, darling, it said.

So I took some of the last of the funds and went up to New York and sat in a cheap hotel room and made contact with Harry. I showed him what I had. His eyes glistened even while he tried to tell me they were junk. I gave him the one that looked least valuable to me. We settled for seven per cent as his end. It took him a day and a half. He brought me back thirty-eight hundred and thirteen dollars. He got rid of two more the next day, one at a time, at a little over four thousand apiece for me. A full day for the next one. Five thousand and a bit. When I turned over the last one, I had a hunch I would not see him again, so I told him I had been holding out the cream of the little crop. He wanted to see it. I told him he could see it when he came back with the money for the fifth one. It made a serious problem for him. He did not know just how to manage his own greed. So he came back, again with a little over five thousand. He didn't look sufficiently disappointed when I told him there wasn't any more. So I knew he had covered all bets. I had covered mine too. Leaving Harry to batter his way out of the bathroom, I had the elevator boy, greased with a ten, take me to the basement where a slightly more expensive fellow, prearranged, let me out a back way into a narrow alley. Forty minutes later I was on a train to Philadelphia, and from there I arranged air transit to Florida.

On an afternoon in late September I had the brown-eyed, sad-eyed blonde come over to the *Busted Flush*. Draperies muted the light in the lounge. She wore a blue dress faded by many washings, and came shyly out of the blaze heat of the day into the coolness of the lounge, wearing her blue dress and her humble company manners, moving well on those shapely, sinewy dancer's legs.

"I call you and you trot right over, just like that, Cathy?"

"I guess so."

"You're a very humble gal, aren't you?"

"I don't know. I guess so. You tried to help

out, Mister. I'm right sorry about that woman. I told you so before, I guess you remember. I'm sorry it had to come about that way."

Her shy oblique glance caught me and moved away. She looked down at her hands. I guess she knew about drunken men. Maybe she could understand the reasons for the drinks I had taken. Maybe she had heard it all in my voice when I had called her to come over.

"Your sympathy touches my heart," I said.

She sighed deeply. "You can talk ugly if it suits you. I don't mind. Seems like nothing comes out right for any person any more these days."

She was sitting on the yellow couch. I picked up a small table and took it over and put it down in front of her. I went and locked the door and then went into the master stateroom and came out with the money. As I had planned, I put it in three piles on the table. A big pile and two slender ones.

"During the fun and games," I said, "Junior spilled the goodies. He got some back and went down with them. There was one time when I could have hauled him in, dead, and picked him clean, the wet money and what other stones he had, and let him sink again. I didn't have the stomach for it. In fact, I didn't even think of it. I got five stones. The rest went overboard. I sold them in New York. I got a total of twenty-two thousand six hundred and sixty-eight dollars for them. There's sixteen hundred and sixty-eight dollars in this pile right here."

She looked at it and looked up at me, eyes as attentive and obedient as a learning child.

"It will cover my expenses," I said. "I spent about that much. This pile is one thousand dollars. I'm taking it as a fee. That leaves twenty thousand in this pile. Yours."

"You said it would be half for you."

"Cathy, I'm not going to argue with you. It was a lousy recovery. It was peanuts. The fee is for self-respect. It's yours."

"I never could touch that much all at once in my lifetime. You should take half."

"Listen, you idiot woman! How do you know you're not being taken? Maybe I got it all from him. Why should you take my word about anything?"

"You did good. I didn't even know you got a thing. You keep half like we said."

I reached and grabbed her purse. I crammed the money into it and managed to fasten the catch. "I got all I want!"

"There's no call to yell. You want me to have it, I'll take it. And I thank you kindly, Travis."

I kicked the table out of the way and slumped onto the couch beside her. The damned humble, docile, forgiving woman. I wanted to beat her. I wanted to do some ugly thing that would destroy that mute earnestness, that anxiety to please me. I hooked a hand around her neck and pulled her over to me, stroked her body and kissed her roughly. I released her and she sagged back and moistened her lips and stared at me with a little frown between her brows.

"Well?" I said.

"If'n you're telling me you want me, and waiting that I should say yes or no, I guess it would be yes, if it would comfort you some, if you think it's what you want off me. I made bad trouble for you . . . and there isn't much I can do one way or another."

I got up and caught her wrist and pulled her along. She came willingly. I pushed her into the stateroom ahead of me. She looked around the room. I stumbled and sat on the bed. She undid a side zipper on that blue dress and gave me a quick and earnest look as she did so, teeth biting into her underlip, a boyish tousel of blonde hair falling across her forehead, her worried little frown still in place. She pulled the dress off over her head and hung it over the back of a chair. She balanced herself and slipped her shoes off. She wore very plain white nylon underthings, trim panties and a functional-looking bra.

"My God, Cathy," I said, "you're not under any compulsion." She looked blank. "You're not obligated."

"You're hurting, ain't you?" she said, and reached her arms behind her and unhooked the bra.

"Get dressed!"

"What?"

"It was a lousy idea. Get dressed and go."

I saw the tears come then, spilling, but not changing the expression of her face. "You got to know what you want," she said. "I'm not so much. I guess you know that. But drinking and all, you got to know or have somebody tell you."

I stretched out with my back to her. "I'm sorry," I said. "Just take off, will you?"

I listened for some sound. I guess she was standing there staring at me. Then she came around the bed and crawled on from the other side, came crawling into my arms, in just her little white pants, tugging and fitting my arms around her, hitching up so she could pull my face into the soft hollow of her throat. She smelled soapy-clean, and faintly of some flower perfume.

"Cathy, I didn't mean . . ."

"Hush up," she said. "It don't have to be that, I know. What you want to do, you want to smash and kick and fight. I know about that, honey. I know about something else too. You got to let go. It's hard to let go. God love you, I know that. A woman can cry it off some. But you listen. I'm just somebody close right now, for you to hold to, and that he'ps too. It don't matter what you want or don't want, or do or don't do. You just hang on close, and you try to let her go. She's gone. You got to let her go the rest of the way, with no blaming yourself. I'm here with you. Just somebody to be with. You can use me just to hang onto, or

love me or whip me or cry some if you could.
Or talk about her or anything. I'll be with you
now. I'm off tonight. Now you think for a
minute and say go or stay."

"I guess . . . stay."

"Sure, honey."

With her free hand, with strong fingers, she
worked at the tension in the nape of my neck,
in the muscles of my shoulders. I did not
realize how tense I had been until from time to
time I sighed and at each long exhalation I
seemed to settle and soften against her.

In the last of daylight I took her hand and
looked at it, at the weathered back of it, the
little blue veins, the country knuckles. It
seemed a very dear hand indeed. I kissed her,
and felt the little ridge where they'd stitched
my mouth. Her brown eyes glinted in the last
of the light, and in a little while her breathing
quickened. It was all strange and deep and
sweet and unemphatic, as though it was an
inescapable extension of that comforting
closeness, as natural as all the rest of it.

In darkness she said in a murmurous voice,
"With that money, I should be near my boy. It
will last good and long down to Candle Key. I
could spell Christine, watching over the kids.
She wants a waitress job again, tired of being
alone there. I can give notice. Honey, what you
should do, you should come on down there in
this boat and tie on up to our old dock down
there. Put you to work, on handyman stuff
that's piled up. With the other kids in school,

we could maybe take Davie fishing in the skiff sometimes. What we could be . . . I guess is a comfort to one another for a time down there, just sweet and close like this was, and we would know when it was time for you to leave. It wouldn't be no obligation to you, Travis."

And so we did. And I was mended as much as I could ever expect. And left finally, wondering if I was not perhaps the world's fool for not settling for that, for keeps.

On the late November day when I left, she grinned away tears, made our jokes which had become familiar to us, and stood on the dock holding the kid's hand, waving until I was past the island and out of sight.

About the Author

JOHN D. MacDONALD, says *The New York Times*, "is a very good writer, not just a good 'mystery writer.' " His Travis McGee novels have established their hero as a modern-day Sam Spade and, along with MacDonald's more than 500 short stories and other bestselling novels—60 in all, including *Condominium* and *The Green Ripper*—have stamped their author as one of America's best all-round contemporary storytellers.